The Thought Scare

and other stories with a philosophical edge

by Leslie Stevenson

ISBN: 978-1-304-67907-9

Copyright © 2013 Leslie Stevenson

All rights reserved, including the right to reproduce this book, or portions thereof in any form. No part of this text may be reproduced, transmitted, downloaded, decompiled, reverse engineered, or stored, in any form or introduced into any information storage and retrieval system, in any form or by any means, whether electronic or mechanical without the express written permission of the author.

This is a work of fiction. Names and characters are the product of the author's imagination and any resemblance to actual persons, living or dead, is entirely coincidental.

PublishNation. London

www.publishnation.co.uk

Preface

I have written and rewritten these stories over the past ten years or so, since retiring as an academic philosopher at the University of St.Andrews. But potential readers can be reassured that they don't need to know anything about philosophy, and that the somewhat unorthodox theology that comes into the title story hardly reappears until the lengthy last story, in which Heaven turns out to be not all it is cracked up to be. Nos. 2 to 4 form a trilogy set in the mythical ancient Kingdom of Jujubia, where the royal family were held in reverential awe. Nos. 8 to 13 are located in Scotland, which may or may not contribute to their alcoholic strength, but perhaps (like the water that goes into the whisky) the setting contributes a distinctive flavour. No. 12 is a blundering attempt at Burns-inspired doggerel (at least it is short!).

A little philosophy enters in unobtrusively here and here, but more obviously in the last two stories. No. 13, a playscript, has deliberate echoes from Plato - his cynical character Thrasymachus in Book I of *The Republic*, and themes from his Socratic dialogues *Symposium, Phaedrus* and *Meno* - but you don't need to know that to enjoy the story (I hope). No. 14, which goes on for nearly 10,000 words, tries to imagine Heaven, and its problems which are not usually thought about; the cast of characters includes St.Peter, St.Paul, guardian angels on the phone, C.S.Lewis, and a touch of Monty Python.

No. 9 was published in *Debut* in 2012, and an earlier version of no. 13 was published by *The Philosopher's Magazine* back in 1999.

1. The Theology of Scarecrows

2. The Emperor Butterfly

3. The Song of the Jubjub Birds

4. The Taming of the Bandersnatch

5. Which Doctor?

6. Gate Zero

7. A Lift to the Spirit

8. Nematode Island

9. Time Train

10. A Taste of Terror

11. The Wind from the Cairngorms

12. Sauciehall Street

13. From Athens to the North

14. Good Heavens!

1. THE THEOLOGY OF SCARECROWS

Half-way through the family meal Billy broke his usual silence:

"Oh Mum, there was a phone call for you - something about scarecrows."

"Scarecrows? What have I to do with scarecrows? Are you sure you got that right?"

"I think so. She said it clearly."

"Who was *she*?"

"Eliza."

"Eliza who?"

"Someth'n beginn'n wif D."

Billy was chewing the last of his shepherd's pie.

"Billy, I've told you not to talk with your mouth full. When you've finished chewing and swallowed, speak to me properly. ... What was her surname?"

"... Doodlebug or something."

"Doodlebug!" exploded Jocelyn, "there can't be a name like that!"

"It would be a wonderful name for a deeply rural place like this", remarked her Dad, who had been deeply immersed in his portion of pie.

"Better keep out of this, Bob", said Jean, sharply.

1

Billy was now getting up to go.

"Hey - don't escape, young man! Don't you want any dessert?"

"No thanks, Mum. I'll just go and chill out."

"Not yet, you won't. We haven't got to the bottom of this Eliza yet."

Jean's three listeners looked at each other for a moment, then fell about with laughter and glee.

"Ahem, let me rephrase that. Has anyone any idea who this Eliza could be?"

There followed a pensive silence, broken only by a moo from the cattle in the back field just behind the house. Then Jocelyn piped up:

"There was that lady at Sunday School."

"Oh, of course - Lady Dubouglay."

"Eliza Whinnyford Dubouglay, Chairperson of the Parochial Church Council", said Bob. "Her ancestors have been landowners here for centuries, and her middle name is the village itself. You're into deep waters, Jean."

"Well, I'm making progress. Did you get her number, Billy?"

"Nope", he said, halfway through the door.

"I thought an eleven-year-old would have more sense."

The rest of the eleven-year-old disappeared.

"It'll be in the Parish Magazine", said Bob.

After the washing up, Jean plucked up courage to phone the formidable Chairperson of the PCC.

"Lady Dubouglay? This is Jean Gregson. Did you leave a message with my son? He said it was something about scarecrows - but could that be right?"

"Oh yes indeed. How good of you to ring back, Jean - and do call me Eliza. I remember having your Jocelyn in Sunday School. What a pretty little girl! But we haven't seen her recently."

"Er ... well ... she's been busy with her other activities."

"Yes that's what they all say", said Eliza, sadly. "Anyway, our new project is precisely designed to involve the younger generation in our church activity. The PCC have decided on a Scarecrow Festival. Each family can create its own scarecrow, and bring them to the Harvest Thanksgiving."

"That sounds great for the kids, but where do *I* come into it?"

"Well, Jean, the PCC thought you would be an excellent person to join us on the Scarecrow Committee. We need people to go round the parish and encourage their neighbours in the construction of scarecrows."

"Well, Lady Dubouglay - Eliza, I mean - I've had some bad experiences with committees ... Can I think about it?"

"Certainly. But don't think too long, Jean. The PCC wants to get these scarecrows moving."

"I thought scarecrows were stationary. ... Oh I'm sorry, I didn't mean to be frivolous."

"The PCC is never frivolous" announced Eliza, "this is a project to reconnect the Church with its people."

"Of course. I'll let you know, then."

"Very well. Good evening, Jean."

At the next family meal Jean announced: "Do you know, there's a plan to have scarecrows all over the village."

"Cool", exclaimed Billy.

"*Whose* plan?" said Bob, sceptically.

"Eliza's - or the PCC's."

"That *means* Eliza. But where will the scarecrows come from?"

"Every family will make their own, and bring them to the Harvest Service."

"So it's a sneaky way of getting people into church."

"I don't see what's sneaky about it. Everyone will be invited, that's all."

"Yes, let's have a scarecrow! We could dress him up", exclaimed Jocelyn; and Billy blurted out:

"Yeah! We could make it scary enough to scare everyone, not just crows."

"I'm not so sure about that", said Jean. "What would the neighbours think?"

"But why did Eliza phone *you*?" asked Bob.

"They want me to join the Scarecrow Committee."

"Ah, there lies the rub. Stay away from village committees, I say - remember what happened last time."

"Yes I know, many hours of boredom, and when I eventually came up with an idea, someone was so rude to me that I walked out."

"Well then, you could tell Eliza scarecrows are not your *field*!"

"Oh very witty! But I don't think she'd be impressed. Actually, that rude old codger has passed on, bless his rude old soul. And a one-off Scarecrow Committee should be different."

Billy exclaimed: "A committee of scarecrows? Go for it Mum, you'd be great!"

"Thank you for that backhanded compliment, Billy."

Eliza was delighted to hear that Jean would join the Committee. Under her masterly chairpersonship the Scarecrow Project moved swiftly forward. Articles appeared in the Parish Magazine and the local paper, and notices were posted all round Whinnyford. The villagers were encouraged to exercise their imagination and ingenuity on the design, engineering, and apparel of scarecrows. The Committee members dutifully pushed leaflets through letter-boxes, cottage windows and farmhouse doors, and did their best to convince sceptics of the benefits of 'recreational scarecrows', as Bob described them. By the mid- September, figures of many shapes and colours had sprung up in gardens, hedges and fields. The Gregson family overruled Billy's penchant for the scary, but endorsed Jocelyn's enthusiasm for dressing up: Jean persuaded Bob to sacrifice an old suit she had been nagging him about for years, and the result was an unusually formal scarecrow in black suit, collar and tie.

Some of the Whinnyford creations conformed to the conventional ragged straw-stuffed stereotype - but there also appeared celebrity scarecrows, erotic scarecrows, and horror scarecrows. Outside the Three Feathers pub stood a crudely-sculpted Kate Duchess of Cambridge, and in May Street there was a Wayne Rooney complete with football. The council estate sported an outsize topless female, rather like those prehistoric obese Venuses that sometimes turn up in the ploughed soil. And the notorious Stuckley family had the affrontery to stick up an imitation of the shameless giant inscribed in the chalk hillside at Cerne Abbas in Dorset, complete with erect male member. Elsewhere there was a Tyrannosaurus Rex, and a giant tarantula.

Inevitably there came mutterings that these tasteless creations were lowering the tone of the village. Letters of complaint were published in the paper, and the new vicar, the Rev. Beatrice Saltmire, was overwhelmed with irate phone calls and emails. She felt she had to raise the issue with the Chairperson of the PCC, though after only one year in the parish she felt somewhat intimidated by Eliza. (Someone at theological college had remarked that the PCC usually provides excellent opportunities for loving your enemies.) However Eliza herself was equally worried about the situation, and readily agreed to convene an emergency meeting of the Scarecrow Committee.

Concern was also rising in the Gregson household. Jocelyn had come home from school crying because she thought scarecrows were chasing her.

"I was walking up May Street past the Tyrannosaurus and the bug-eyed alien, and I heard them growling at me."

"Don't worry, Jos", said Billy, "I know those lads in May Street. They were just having a bit of fun".

"But then I saw the scarecrows coming *towards* me", cried Jocelyn, "and I got really scared."

"Are you sure you weren't imagining it?" asked Bob.

"How could I imagine a thing like that?" wailed Jocelyn.

Jean intervened: "This scarecrow business is getting out of hand. I'm not having my daughter coming home frightened like this." She phoned Eliza, and was relieved to hear of the emergency committee meeting the next evening.

In the draughty back room of the Village Hall, the meeting began with the customary prayer, after which a point of order was raised by Mr. James Twiddles, concerning whether the Vicar was a full member of the Scarecrow Committee, which was technically a sub-committee of the PCC. Though the Vicar was of course an *ex officio* member of the PCC, Twiddles wondered whether it followed that she was on every sub-committee. Several pairs of eyes were raised to heaven - and heaven responded in the penetrating voice of Lady Eliza:

"Good gracious, Mr. Twiddles, have you nothing better to do with that brilliant mind of yours? We have serious business tonight, and we need the Vicar here. If there is any doubt about the matter, we can co-opt her here and now. All those in favour?"

More than enough hands went up to quell the doubts of Twiddles.

"Now then", said Eliza, "there is just one substantive item on our agenda, namely the future of our Scarecrow Project. A large number of complaints have been received about the scarecrows that some people have seen fit to display. You have all seen what I mean."

There were mutterings round the table:

"Quite disgusting, some of them!"

"Not fit to appear in church".

Jean put in a brave word: "We did encourage people to be creative".

"But these scarecrows are not creative, they're just following the worst examples in the mass media", said James, sourly and virtuously

"Hasn't popular art always been imitative?"

"Maybe, but the Church cannot lend its approval to such stuff."

"I'm not keen on it myself, any more than you, but *we started* this project, and some of us went round positively badgering people to take part. We can hardly complain when they respond."

The Vicar judiciously intervened: "Jean has a point. And we might remember that in the past the Church has encouraged some pretty gruesome images. Think of the gargoyles on our own church!"

"You're surely not suggesting, Vicar, that we can bring those disgraceful scarecrows into our Harvest service?" said Eliza. "But what else can we do with them?" she added, with unusual uncertainty.

"Maybe we should select those scarecrows that are *fit* for church?" suggested Peter Pluck, a clerk from the council office who typically contributed one remark per meeting.

"So some scarecrows would be more equal than others?" asked Jean. "If we refuse entry to some, we'd be offending the very people we were trying to attract."

"Yes", said Beatrice, "we meant to be inclusive."

At this point Peter unexpectedly found his second wind: "Suppose we invite them all to the field behind the Church instead? We could have a scarecrow party."

"Peter, you're a genius!" cried Beatrice. "Make that a *bonfire* party - a bonfire of the vanities, indeed. We can burn the scarecrows on the Saturday night before Harvest Festival Service."

"We could call it 'Wicker Night'", suggested Jean.

"What's that?" asked Eliza suspiciously.

"Oh, it's some film my kids watched, in which straw men get burnt."

"Well", said Eliza, grandly, "it's not what we first thought of, but it would be a fitting end for those grotesques. And perhaps it *would* appeal to the popular imagination."

"If I remember right, there *was* ritual burning of straw figures in pagan times", said James.

"So we have ancient precedent for the idea!" said Jean brightly.

"But that was pagan, not Christian", objected Eliza.

"The early Church incorporated practices from the preceding culture, provided they were harmless", replied Beatrice.

A short silence followed, broken by that overplayed Mozart theme from Twiddles' mobile phone, which he hastily silenced. Then Eliza said, "I think we have the answer to our prayers. I always had faith in the divine guidance of our PCC."

So later that week the members of the Scarecrow Committee were to be seen on their rounds again, in glorious Indian summer weather, delivering leaflets with the revised invitation. Excitement grew as the 'wicked' Saturday night drew near. But a few days before, Jean's bedside phone rang at 11 pm:

"Good evening, Jean, this is your local scarecrow speaking. I'm getting lonely standing in my field all night, after I've done my day job scaring the crows. But I've been watching *you* going past with your leaflets, and I've been thinking how lovely you look in your flowery dress with the autumn sun shining through …"

"Who is that? Is this supposed to be a joke?"

"No, I'm just a lonesome old scarecrow, and I wish you would come up my field and see me sometime …"

Jean slammed the phone down.

"What was *that* about?" asked Bob.

She went pink in the face, swallowed, and said: "That was sexual harassment from a scarecrow."

Bob started to laugh, but then he saw she was trembling - quite unusually for her.

"I'm going to ring the police," she announced.

"Steady on, old girl, it might only be someone's idea of a joke. But if it happens again, we might take action."

Jean thought for a moment, calmed down a bit, and said "Maybe. But I'm not going to take this lying down."

The phone did indeed ring again, at the same time the next night. Jean picked it up, winked at Bob, and said in her firmest tone of voice:

"Jean Gregson here."

"Jean darling, I'm stuck in the middle of this field, and I can't get near you. If you would only come up here, I could breathe in your fragrance. You could help me off my pole, and I could get out my other pole ..."

"... and I would grab you by that other pole, swing you round my head, and hurl you into the furthest corner of the field, where you would crumble into an untidy little pile of rags and straw."

It was the amorous scarecrow who rang off this time. Bob congratulated Jean on her choice of words. They agreed that the scarecrow theme had become too deeply implanted in the minds of the inmates of Whinnyford, and the sooner the whole thing went up in smoke the better.

But the next night something else happened. Bob went down to the pub for a few glasses with his mates, and walked home up the road as usual. But this time he stumbled through the front door with a bleeding forehead, meeting Billy on his way to bed.

"Dad, what happened?" cried Billy. The alarm in his voice brought Jean running from the kitchen.

"Oh my God! Have you been in a fight? You'll have to stop going to that pub, I never did like it."

"No, no, the pub was fine - but something strange happened on the way home," said Bob, holding a reddening handkerchief to his head.

"Come to the bathroom and I'll clean you up", said Jean. "And Billy, you're supposed to be in bed."

"But I want to hear what happened to Dad. Was it to do with scarecrows?"

"Scarecrows, my foot. I'm up to here with scarecrows. Go to bed this minute."

Jean took Bob to the bathroom, but Billy was able to overhear their conversation from his bed.

"It's only a superficial cut. You'll live - but you'll be a scarface for a while."

"Ah well, I always fancied myself as a pirate."

"You've had one pint too many. And your breath smells of beer and smoke - not my sort of pirate."

"But scars and bad breath is what pirates *do*." And Bob moved to give his wife a kiss on the lips, but she stepped quickly aside.

"Pirates, scarecrows … what is this place coming to? Come on then, tell me what really happened."

"Actually, Billy's right, it did involve scarecrows - at least I thought so. I was walking up our road, perhaps just a tiny bit unsteadily, in the light of that beautiful harvest moon. I was thinking what a peaceful place this is to live, in the depths of the country, when I had a sort of feeling I was being followed. I glanced around, and saw nobody. There was no traffic, no footsteps, just the distant hoot of an owl. I looked again, and I thought I saw some dark upright shapes moving in the fields - they certainly weren't cattle or horses. The hairs on my neck began to rise. I looked round a third time, and now there seemed to be two huge scarecrows creeping silently through the fields behind me: on the right was a King Kong, and on the left was a Gordon Brown."

"You obviously had *two* pints too many," interrupted Jean, "this scarecrow business is going to everybody's heads."

"I only had the usual two - honest. I hate to admit it, but I broke into a run. Then I tripped and fell on my face, and when I got up the visions had vanished."

There was a snigger from Billy's room, and Bob went straight in.

"Were you listening to that, Billy?"

"Sorry Dad, I couldn't help hearing."

"You were supposed to be asleep. Do *you* know anything about moving scarecrows?"

"No, Dad. I'm sure it was the village boys frightening Jos, but God knows what's going on at night. Maybe we need something to scare away the scarecrows."

"Now *there's* an idea. We'll talk about it tomorrow. Good night Billy, you need your sleep."

At breakfast they had to fill in Jocelyn on the story behind the sticking plaster on her Dad's forehead, which only made her even more nervous about scarecrows. Then Bob returned to Billy's idea of the night before:

"Billy suggested we need a *meta*scarecrow."

"What's that?" asked Jocelyn.

"Well, a scarecrow scares away crows, but a metascarecrow would scare away other scarecrows."

"What on earth could do that?" asked Jean.

A deep silence followed, and the grandfather clock in the hall ticked ponderously.

"How about Jesus on the cross?" said Billy, out of the blue.

"Good God, no", said Jean.

"Well, if you think about it, that *is* a pretty scary idea - a man dying in agony, for hours", observed Bob.

"But it's such a holy image. Wouldn't people object?"

"Why not check it out with the Vicar?"

So Jean phoned Beatrice, who could see no problem about people putting crucifixes in their gardens if they wished. So Billy and Jocelyn stripped their scarecrow of his suit, leaving only a loincloth, and rehung him with nails through hands and feet. (Bob was tempted to redeem his sacrificed suit, but Jean vetoed that.)

That very evening there was a phone call from Eliza: "I see you have replaced your scarecrow by a crucifix."

"Yes, it was Billy's idea. We asked Beatrice, and she said it was all right", replied Jean defensively.

"Far be it from me to question anything the Vicar says, but did you realize we can hardly put a crucifix on a bonfire?"

"Oh dear, we didn't think of that."

"I will have to take the matter up with the Vicar."

Next time the phone rang it was Beatrice herself:

"Jean dear, I don't know if your family were thinking of burning your crucified scarecrow, but the symbolism doesn't feel right - don't you agree?"

"Oh my God! Yes, of course. We forgot all about the bonfire when we had that idea."

"Imagine the headlines in the press: 'Vicar burns crucifix'. I could consult the Bishop, but I'm pretty sure he'd say no. And to be frank I'd rather not draw his attention to our Wicker Night, I suspect he might not entirely approve."

"That's quite all right, Beatrice, our family has no enthusiasm for burning. We can just quietly dispose of our crucifix."

"But you can do better than that, Jean. It could be the one scarecrow brought into church the next morning - to atone for the others, as it were. Your children could carry it in. I'm sure the Bishop would like *that*."

"No doubt he would, but whether Billy and Jos would is another matter."

"Would you like me to ask them?"

"Why not? I'll bring them to the phone."

Beatrice explained her idea to Billy and Jocelyn, and was met with embarrassed silence. Jean, listening in on the extension, prompted:

"Go on, Billy, say something to the Vicar".

"What's so special about Jesus, anyway?" he suddenly asked.

"Well, Billy, you're raising one of the biggest questions of all", said Beatrice, "and people have argued about it for centuries. But we know that he went around healing people in body and mind, and teaching them how to find new spiritual life. Somehow that got him into trouble with the authorities, and he was condemned to death. But what he believed in has survived, and the Christian churches have been inspired by him ever since. That's why your crucified scarecrow is so special, and why we'd very much like it if you and Jocelyn would carry him up to the front of the church next Sunday morning, after the others been burnt."

After a thoughtful interval, Billy said "OK then."

"Is that all right with *you*, Jocelyn?" asked Beatrice.

"Can we just take him up to the front, and then go back to our Mum and Dad?"

"Yes, of course", said Beatrice. "Fantastic. That's settled, then."

When Wicker Saturday came round at last, all the Whinnyford scarecrows were to be seen converging onto Potters Field, immediately behind the Parish Church, where they were posted in a circle, with the Gregsons' crucifix in the centre to Christianize the event. The Scarecrow Committee had arranged for a barbecue, a hot dog stall, and a soft drinks outlet - but cans of beer and lager also found their unofficial way into the field, in some numbers. Over the loudspeakers came a tasteful selection of music including Handel's Fireworks Suite, courtesy of James Twiddles.

There was a glorious blaze of orange in the sky as the sun set over Otterby Wood, and the rooks in the trees cawed as people munched and mingled. Beatrice eagerly took the opportunity to greet many who had never been seen on church ground before, including even the colorfully-tattooed Stuckley family. Just after sunset, she took up a loud-hailer:

"Good evening, and a very warm welcome to everyone. It looks like we have the whole community of Whinnyford here. I won't keep you long from your hot dogs and liquid refreshment …"

Cheers and shouts arose.

"... and in a few minutes we will start the fiery part of the evening"

Louder cheers.

"... but I thought this special event deserves just a few words."

"Not too many", said some wit - or twit.

"Your scarecrow creations are more manifold and imaginative than the PCC ever dreamed of ..."

Chortles and cheers.

"We can see them as representing our imperfect human nature, our desires and fears, our idols and ideals - and our immersion in the culture of our time."

Silence.

"Don't get me wrong. I'm not saying it's bad, I'm just saying it's *mixed*, like everything in human life. Good, bad, and indifferent are muddled up together. But we have to discriminate. We need to discern what is best, and that isn't always obvious. And we need to *do* what's best - that's the hardest part ..."

Deeper silence, with some restiveness from the lager drinkers.

"The Church over the centuries has tried to help people to discern what is good, and to follow it, and we're still here today for the same purpose. That's all I have to say tonight. It only remains to thank our hard-working Scarecrow Committee for organizing this gloriously successful event ..."

Polite applause.

"... and to ask them to start the conflagration of the scarecrows. You may see this as a purgation of the unacceptable parts of ourselves. The crucifix will remain, and will be brought into church tomorrow morning, to represent all our cares and scares."

Loud whoops all round the field - though whether for conflagration or for purgation it was impossible to tell.

"Not much about God in what you said", observed Eliza, standing beside Beatrice.

"Oh, Eliza! It's implicit. Doesn't it come to the same thing in different language, with symbolism and imagery? The heresy-hunters can come after me if they must, but we've got to reach out to all humanity, haven't we?"

The moment had at last come for Peter Pluck to go round with a glowing wand to ignite the scarecrows. Their mixture of straw, wood, rags and plastic caught fire readily, and soon most of them were ablaze. Then the Scarecrow Committee got another surprise. From the ears of an Elvis-lookalike, green sparks began spraying into the night air, and Catherine wheels revolved on the nipples of the bug-eyed alien (if aliens have nipples). Many more scarecrows turned out to have fireworks concealed on their persons (if scarecrows have persons). All this added to the gaiety of the occasion; and when someone changed Twiddles' classical selection to something with a heavy beat, the assembled congregation began to dance around the circle of combusting scarecrows, and the scene looked like *Walpurgisnacht* in middle England 2013.

There remained one final shock. When the fire reached the shameless giant and got to his erect phallus, there was a loud whoosh, and a rocket shot up out of it. People whooped with glee, and all eyes followed it into the sky. At the top of its trajectory it ejaculated a stream of whirring blue particles, with a loud pop. Then its smouldering remains drifted down towards the church, landed on the roof, and slid down into the gutter, where wind-blown hay had accumulated. Flames shot up immediately, and were fanned by the rising breeze. Soon the roof itself was alight, and though a chain of men tried to get water from the nearby river, they had nothing bigger to hand than beer glasses. By the time the Fire Brigade arrived, the fifteenth century church was beyond salvation.

After hurried consultations overnight, the morning's Harvest Festival was relocated to the Methodist Church. With two congregations united, plus many faces not seen in either before, the unpretentious brick building was full to bursting, and for the first time in living memory there was standing room only in a religious service in Whinnyford. At the start, Billy and Jocelyn solemnly carried in their crucified and smoke-stained metascarecrow. (Beatrice had had to remind them to collect it from the field, where it had been left in the chaos of the night.)

There wasn't a sermon as such, but before the last hymn Beatrice made a speech that went down in village memory:

"We are immensely grateful to our Methodist friends for being good Samaritans and providing us with a home in adversity. Over the last few weeks we have witnessed a burgeoning of village life and creativity, and last night we had a purgation, much more than we bargained for. The loss of our medieval church was indeed a sort of death. But it is my belief that there can be a resurrection! For remember, the Church is not a building, it is *the people*. Look how many of us are here - we are a community that cares about its past and its future. So we can already begin to envisage a new creation. Not, I suggest, a mock-medieval building - we should respect our past, but we don't have to copy it. Let us imagine a state-of-the-art village centre, with a main space for worship open to various denominations and faiths, and a smaller room for aerobics, pottery classes, music and whatever other decent activities people get up to round here. And there should be a non-alcoholic café, something of which we have long felt the need - and toilets, to which the same applies. There will have to be fundraising of course, but we all know that we have a very capable PCC."

After the service, Ned Stuckley of the shaven pate and black tee shirt came up to Beatrice, who warmly shook his hand, tattooed with a scorpion though it was.

"We're so sorry, Vicar", he said. "We only meant a bit of fun, we never dreamt the church would burn down."

"Ah, but our actions so often have unintended consequences."

"Can you ever forgive us?"

"As we said in the service, God always forgives those who truly repent. And that reminds me, didn't someone tell me you're in the building trade? Perhaps you could contribute your skills to the reconstruction project?"

So ended one memorable episode in the long rural history of Whinnyford, and so began another.

2. THE EMPEROR BUTTERFLY

Once upon a time, in the beautiful and exotic land of Jujubia where the Royal Family were held in reverential awe, there went out an Imperial Decree, in the interest of a modest increase in the Gross National Blissfulness, that there should be a Tasteful Promotion of Eco-Tourism. The most eminent biologists of Jujubia were consulted as to which species of the country's manifold wildlife might be most attractive to the discerning visitor. When they presented their humble report to the newly-created Ministry of Esteemed Guests, at the top of their list was the magnificent Emperor Butterfly. It was recommended not just for its large size and iridescent purple wings, but for its value as a symbol of the Emperor himself and thus of the nation as a whole.

Thus it came to pass that Wiobe, who had hitherto occupied the lowly role of Deputy Assistant Royal Forester, was entrusted with the task of constructing a nature walk with information boards at selected stations, to guide esteemed pilgrims on the Emperor Butterfly Trail. He was given the title "His Majesty's Interpreter of Butterflies", and was provided with compendious information on their lifestyle by the National Panel of Lepidopterists.

So, on a typically beautiful Jujubian morning, with fluffy white clouds sailing over the foothills of the great mountains, and the Jubjub birds (second on the National Ecological List) calling plaintively to their mates, Wiobe set out with his carefully-prepared information boards and his trusty mallet, ready to install them at the preselected spots. The first post went in smoothly, and Wiobe hummed happily to himself as he walked up the trail to station no.2. He was about to hammer the second notice into place when he noticed that a little crowd of locals had already gathered around the first one, a couple of hundred yards downhill. What is more, they were pointing and giggling, then they held their sides, and two of them quite literally fell to the ground laughing uproariously. Wiobe was suddenly alarmed: such behaviour was quite out of the national character, yet it seemed to have something to do with his own honest and conscientious work. He glanced at the board in his hand, which read:

EMPEROR BUTTERFLY TRAIL
STATION NO. 1: Feeding habits

The Emperor Butterfly, symbol of our sacred land of Jujubia and of our revered Royal Family, lives entirely on liquid in its short but magnificent life of flight. The mature insects can be observed alighting on the Kaliscus plants and inserting their long probosci (feeding tubes) into the centre of the flowers. The nectar which they thus imbibe fuels their energetic flutterings over these fertile flower-bedecked meadows.

Wiobe realized that in the excitement and enthusiasm of his august new calling he had installed Information Board no.2 at Station no.1. But why was it provoking such uncouth mirth? He recalled its wording, which he could readily remember since he had spent so much time composing it. Indeed he had rather prided himself on his eloquence:

EMPEROR BUTTERFLY TRAIL
STATION NO. 2: Mating habits

On hot afternoons in June, you may, if you are lucky, observe how our national symbol goes about the delicate business of reproduction. The Emperor and Empress chase across the sky, making whirligig patterns around each other, their purple robes glinting in the sunshine. If you are sharp-eyed, you can distinguish the Empress by the width of her body. When their energetic courtship reaches a sufficient degree of excitement, the Empress will perch on a Kaliscus flower. The Emperor, if his ardour remains keen, will fly in on top of her and grip her round the middle with his six legs. With iridescent wings fluttering in unison, their bodies will curve elegantly, then touch. Though you cannot see it except through a microscope, a small packet of

imperial genes is transmitted (if all goes well). There may be a quivering of ecstasy, though this does not happen on all occasions, and soon afterwards the wedded pair will part. This process may be repeated with several Emperors in succession, who appear to find it extremely taxing, for they flap off weakly afterwards, and some have even been observed to drop down dead. The thoroughly impregnated Empress will then seek out the leaves of the Wakacious plant on which to lay her fertilized eggs and start the new generation.

Wiobe knew immediately that his life was in danger, so he dropped his tools and fled the country. He walked briskly uphill, trying to be inconspicuous; he kept going into the foothills, then up and up into the mountains, pausing only to slake his thirst from the ice-cold streams. Eventually he crossed a high snowy pass into the alien land of Bizarristan, where he lived rather less happily ever after.

3. THE SONG OF THE JUBJUB BIRDS

Once upon a time in the beautiful and exotic land of Jujubia where the Royal Family were held in reverential awe, there occurred a minor ecological crisis. Spring came round, the snow melted off the foothills of the great mountains and lavishly irrigated the Jujubian forests and meadows. The Kaliscus plants sprouted enormous buds which promised a particularly rich display of nectar for the Emperor Butterflies to gorge on later in the year. And yet that spring, the Jubjub birds did not begin to sing.

I should explain that these birds were also held in reverence in Jujubia, being etymologically and mythologically connected with the nation itself. So when they failed to come up with their usual spring song, anxiety spread through the normally placid populace. True, there had been the usual "jub-jub" calls by which the males claim and defend their territories, but neither sex followed up with the plaintive tweets by which they select their mates and reinforce their pair bonds. To those of us brought up on blackbirds and skylarks the "Twa-at/Twee-et" duets of the Jubjub pairs might hardly deserve the title of "song", but they are music in the ears of the denizens of Jujubia, who wait eagerly for them each year as a sign of renewed warmth and fertility.

The Imperial Court had been listening out for the annual twee-ets as avidly as the commoners; for Jujubia was not a place of cities, let alone traffic jams and urban sprawl, indeed the Palace Complex itself backed on to a carefully preserved area of virgin forest in which the Jubjubs always nested. The relationship between national culture and natural environment was so close that any upset in the latter became cause for concern about the former. Thus it was the Grand Vizier convened a meeting of the Council of State to discuss the unaccustomed silence of the Jubjubs. After two hours of grave cogitation, it was decided to send a Deputation to Bolockostra, the oldest and most prestigious shamaness in the land, in the belief that she if anyone would know the secrets of nature and what they portended for Jujubia.

So a Deputation of Three wended its way on muleback over three long days, plodding up many miles of forest tracks until they came in sight of the snowy peaks of the great mountain-range. In the gnarled branches of the largest pine at the very edge of the forest there was a tree house, cunningly and ecologically constructed using the remains of other trees long since dead. There was no stairway or ladder, only a thin rope of vine-stalks. Utter silence prevailed, broken only by gusts of icy wind from the mountains. The Deputation looked at each other in hesitation, then the Speaker pointed to the rope. His Number Three pulled it, and there came a faint rattle from somewhere above. More silence, and the rope shivered in the wind. The Speaker nodded to his Number Two, who yanked more vigorously and repeatedly. At last there was a shuffle and a cough from inside the tree house, and the branches parted to reveal a wizened face, brown as a walnut and framed by wisps of yellowish hair. A cracked voice spoke:

"Who is it that disturbs the peace of Upper Jujubia?"

The Speaker of the Deputation now took up his appointed role:

"Peace be unto you, O Esteemed Bolockostra. We bring you felicitous greetings from the Imperial Court".

"Ah yes, I thought someone might be coming. But how do I know you represent the Court?"

"We have brought you a gift, sanctioned by the Grand Vizier, in the name of the Emperor Himself. Behold ... a chicken!"

Bolockostra's eyes widened. Number Three took out an odorous package from his saddlebag, and tied the rope round it. It ascended quickly, and there were sounds of unpacking and sniffing.

"Normally I'm a vegetarian, but I'll make an exception in this case, since it's from the Emperor. But next time, don't forget the pepper and salt."

The Speaker judged that now was the opportune time to deliver his message:

"The Imperial Court has delegated me to ask you, O Bolockostra, why the Jubjub birds do not sing this spring."

The wrinkled face smiled knowingly:

"Yes, I have noticed that too. But the ways of Nature are deep and unpredictable. Our human knowledge is only of appearances."

"But surely you of all people, O Esteemed Bolockostra, must know the truth of this matter. We all depend on Nature for our very existence. The Council are concerned for the future of the Nation when the Jubjubs do not sing."

The shamaness stared at each of the Three in turn with such piercing eyes that they found it impossible to return her gaze. Then she suddenly muttered:

"Ask the Emperor if he is fulfilling all his duties."

The walnut face disappeared, and the leaves closed behind it. The Speaker said despairingly:

"How can anyone ask the Emperor such a question?"

Numbers Two and Three could offer no answer to that. They yanked the rope in the hope of eliciting further elucidation from the shamaness, but were met with no reply except sounds of enthusiastic munching and the occasional chicken bone thrown to the winds. So there was nothing for it but to make their way back to Court with this impossible suggestion.

When the Deputation of Three made their report to the Council, they were criticized for not making more effort to interrogate Bolockostra, and someone commented that they had made a poor return on the investment of a whole chicken. But after all complaints had been voiced, the facts remained as they were. The advice of the shamaness, chicken or no chicken, still carried weight with the highest in the land of Jujubia. The problem was how to act on it. As far as they were aware, the youthful new Emperor had been scrupulous in the performance of his official duties so far. There could surely be no question of raising even the faintest of doubts about that. But then a hand was shakily raised by the most junior member of the Council, the Recorder of the Back Passage. At this point I need to explain, firstly, that the said Passage is a narrow corridor at the rear of the Palace Complex that connects the Emperor's State Bedchamber to the Empress's Bedroom, and secondly, that the Council, having a legitimate concern in the production of legitimate heirs to the Imperial Throne, had by long-standing convention appointed a Recorder to record the number and dates of conjugal imperial visits. The present occupant of this humble office was a sallow youth of a small size suitable for concealment in a strategically-placed cupboard halfway down the Back Passage. The Grand Vizier glared at him and said:

"Well, Recorder?"

"Your Honour, I hesitate to report, but I have not recorded any visits in the last three weeks."

"Are you sure?"

"Well sir it is hard to be absolutely certain because - you know, sir, my job being what it is, crumpled up in a cupboard all night - I cannot swear that I have remained completely awake *all* the time …"

"Falling asleep on Court Duty? - that would have been a capital offence in olden times. But we have no time for executions now. No visits in two weeks, you say?"

"Yes sir. As far as I could tell. Honest, sir."

The Imperial Council was now presented with two further problems: whether to believe the Recorder's report, and if so, what to do about it. On the whole, the inclination was to believe him, indeed someone asked why have we appointed a Recorder of the Back Passage all these years if we don't take his report seriously, when it matters? The collective wisdom of the Council was impressed by the congruence between the testimony of the Recorder, the upset in Nature, and the words of the shamaness. So the question arose how to approach the Emperor on such a very delicate matter. All eyes turned to the Grand Vizier, three times the age of the young Emperor and with vast experience of matters of State. He realized of course what was being asked of him, and said:

"I will see what I can do. But pray for me."

So at the next private audience between the Emperor and his Grand Vizier, when the former said breezily:

"Well, Viz, what's on the agenda today?"

the latter cleared his throat, and said:

"Sire, the Jubjub birds have not sung this spring".

"What? Those jubby birds? Why yes, I believe you're right! I hadn't noticed. Well, what of it?"

"Sire, you know how important is the balance between our kingdom and Nature. You have already declared yourself a deep ecologist. The Council have been led to believe that a disturbance in Nature reflects an imbalance in our own society".

"Well, what are you getting at? Where is the imbalance you refer to?"

"Sire, we sent a delegation to the shamaness Bolockostra."

"Viz, you surprise me. Should we believe anything that old witch says?"

"Sire, the Council thought it wise to gain all the intelligence we could, from the widest available sources. But you may rest assured that we carefully evaluate whatever intelligence we receive."

"So what is the conclusion of the Council?"

The Vizier now swallowed hard, and said:

"The Council thought we should ask whether all duties are being performed, from the top to the bottom of our sacred land of Jujubia".

"From the top? Do you mean me - your Emperor?"

"Sire, you have yourself acknowledged that we all depend on Nature. In a phrase I have heard elsewhere 'We are all in this together'. So the question applies to us all".

"Am I to understand that the Council is asking me whether I am performing all my duties?"

The Emperor had gone red in the face, and for one terrible moment the Vizier thought he was angry (in former times the Vizier's own head might have been in danger). But then he realized that the Emperor was *blushing*, and judged that this was the appropriate moment to end today's audience:

"Sire, I think I have asked you more than enough for one day. May I humbly take my leave?"

The Emperor was indeed embarrassed, but for not quite the reason that the Council suspected. Some weeks before he had had his first row with his delectable young Empress, and it was all about the colour of the walls in her bedroom. She had chosen "Loquacious Yellow" from the chart of samples that the Imperial Designer had proffered her, and her wish was soon fulfilled by the Imperial Decorators. But after a month of waking with that very loquacious colour she had begun to find it a bit too *loud*, and expressed a wish to have the room repainted. Her loving husband had taken exception to this, saying that since he had so recently succeeded his spendthrift father Jujucious XIII (Revered be his Memory) who had abruptly departed this life after a particularly lavish dinner (the old phrase was 'dying of a surfeit'), he was determined to set an example of simpler living and deficit reduction. At his slimmed down Coronation ceremony he had taken the name of Judicious I, which some had felt a trifle arrogant - though of course no-one would breathe such a thought aloud. His serenely beautiful young Empress Lusciousa had protested that surely the repainting of one room, the one in which they consummated their Sacred Marriage, would not break the Bank of Jujubia. Unfortunately this developed into a battle of wills, and in the stalemate all consummation was put on hold.

This was what made the face of Judicious I redden at his Vizier's words. Left alone in his Audience Chamber, he decided that the marital quarrel had gone far enough, so he made an unannounced visit to his Empress in her Painting Room, where she spent her free time executing delicate watercolours of the landscapes of Jujubia, complete with tastefully-placed peasants. Her Imperial husband now became less imperious, and said:

"Forgive me, dearest, perhaps I've been a little too strict about the redecoration. It's not a matter to break the Bank of Jujubia - nor our hearts either".

Lusciousa smiled with especial serenity, and replied:

"Well, maybe the colour is not so vital. If we are still running a deficit, I can live a little longer with this Loquacious Yellow".

That night the Recorder of the Back Passage was excited to record not one but two conjugal visits, graced by sounds of increased passion. And the very next morning there came the sounds of "Twa-at/Twee-et". The Jubjub birds belatedly took up what passes for their song, and the denizens of Jujubia lived more happily thereafter - for some time, at least.

4. THE TAMING OF THE BANDERSNATCH

Once upon a time in the beautiful and exotic land of Jujubia, where the Royal Family were held in reverential awe, there arose a threat to the felicity of the nation. There had long been a tradition of amateur music-making, and most villages had a little band of enthusiastic pluckers, puffers and bangers, who would perform on their dulcimers, Jujubian bagpipes and leather drums on Sunday afternoons, to the delight (and sometimes to the despair) of their neighbours. But over recent months there had been mysterious disappearances of musicians. Groups would play their hearts out, then vanish into thin air. And it was usually the more tuneful bands that went, so there was danger to the quality as well as the quantity of Jujubian music, not to mention the loss of relatives.

Rumours began to circulate, as they do. An inebriated conversation in the snug of an ancient Jujubian pub went somewhat as follows:

"It's our best players that be goin'. Oi reckon the batter the music, the more likely they'll be taken up to Heaven to entertain the departed souls up there."

"Oh Jammie! Surely Providence would not keep bereaving us of our nearest and dearest so prematurely?"

Deep draughts of strong Jujubian beer were appreciatively and silently swigged, until another idea came to the surface:

"Maybe our musicians are being spirited away by the agents of a foreign power?"

"But Jellie, Jujubia has enjoyed peaceful relations with our neighbours for ages past. And why would *musicians* be selected for extradition?"

The only woman present now announced:

"My little Jujub said he saw something like a giant hand snatch up a band while they were in full flow, and waft them into the sky."

At that the oldest man in Jujubia, well into his second century, woke up suddenly and said in his quavering voice:

"Aye, aye! When Oi was young there was a folk memory that once upon a time - long, long ago - there were giants in this land."

From this slender evidence there grew a common conviction that a monstrous "Bandsnatcher" was at large, with a special taste for music - or for musicians.

The Imperial Council convened several times to discuss the threat to gross national felicity. The latest meeting was graced by the unusual attendance of Emperor Judicious I, who had become personally concerned about national security. After humbly welcoming His Majesty, the Vizier asked him if he wanted to chair the meeting himself, but the Emperor said:

"No, no, just follow your usual procedure. I'll chip in if I have anything to say."

So the Vizier asked:

"Has anyone any new intelligence about the nature of this Bandsnatcher?"

The latest rumours were reported, even some from the numerous pubs, but none of them carried much credence with the Council. Then the Head Administrator of Mules spoke up, addressing the Emperor directly:

"Sire, as a precautionary measure, I humbly suggest that Jujubia should reconvene its muleback army. As we all know, it has been disbanded for some centuries, through a long era of peace. But it has been wisely said that the price of peace is eternal vigilance, and since we now face a threat of unknown magnitude, I would put it to the Council that the time has come to renew our vigilance, in the form of our traditional armoured mules and archers."

No one on the Council ventured to dispute this logic, although some privately thought such a re-armament programme a bit premature. All eyes were directed at the Vizier, whose own eyes looked to his Emperor - who gravely nodded his head and thereby settled the matter.

The Administrator of Mules was a zealous administrator indeed, and starting the very next day, mules were requisitioned from farms, men between the ages of twenty and thirty were called up for archery training, and all available leather was commandeered to make armour (metal being unknown in Jujubia, except for the Imperial Crown). After a week, it was realized that there was nowhere near enough leather to fit out the incipient army, so an urgent programme of cow-culling and tanning was instituted. At the next meeting of the Council, there was a protest on behalf of the agricultural lobby by the Minister of Sustenance:

"This military programme has denuded our farms of their working mules, and now our cows are being slaughtered. If this goes on, crops will not get sown, milk will run out, and we will not be able to guarantee the food supply to the nation."

The Administrator of Mules, who was now acting as *de facto* Chief of the Defence Staff, replied with vehemence:

"There is a threat to our nation. That overrides all other considerations. Our population must be prepared to make sacrifices. There may be blood, toil, tears, and sweat."

At that point the Recorder of the Back Passage, who had matured somewhat since his early appointment to the humble office of recording conjugal visits between Emperor and Empress, felt a rush of blood to his head, and heard himself saying:

"By what authority does the Administrator of Mules demand sacrifices of the nation, and appoint himself head of the army? These matters have not been brought before the whole Council to decide."

There was an aghast silence, in which the members of the Imperial Council pretended to examine their navels, many of which were well cushioned. Then the Vizier said solemnly:

"Of course these are matters for the Council. But we are living through a national emergency; actions must be swiftly taken, and if necessary, approved afterwards. May we take it that the Administrator of Mules is confirmed as Chief of the Defence Staff, with all necessary powers?"

The Overseer of Forests asked:

"And what would those powers be?"

to which the acting Chief replied imperiously:

"Too many questions! Now is the time for action, not words."

So the armament programme continued apace, the price of dairy produce went up, and the children of poorer families had to go without their bedtime milk. However the new recruits began rather to enjoy their training in archery, as a change from the daylong agricultural labour that was their usual lot. In Council the opinion was voiced that the manly arts of war had been neglected for too long. But the threat to national felicity had not been seen off, for the dwindling number of amateur musicians suffered further depredations. Another meeting of the Council was summoned to decide how to *use* the muleback army that was now approaching readiness. The obvious questions were raised (rather belatedly, some thought) by the National Lepidopterist, of all people:

"What do we know about the nature of the threat that faces us? If there is really such a thing as a Bandsnatcher, from where does it come? And where does it take our musicians? What does it do with them? Can we track its movements? What weaponry would be effective against it?"

"Indeed, we are somewhat lacking in intelligence," observed the Vizier.

"Yes, in both senses of the word", said the Recorder of the Back Passage - but only to himself, and disguised it with a cough.

The Imperial Interior Designer now put in his pennyworth:

"We must cast our net of surveillance and intelligence as widely as possible. We could consult the shamaness Bolockostra, as we have on previous occasions of national crisis."

The more freethinking members of the Court doubted whether a shamaness would be a reliable source of intelligence, but for lack of anything better, it was resolved to send a deputation to her.

Because of the unknown danger, the usual Committee of Three was accompanied by a security detail of six mule-mounted archers. With full leather armour covering both man and beast, they looked like centaurs - except that the equine part was mule rather than horse, which made them slow of foot (and it must be confessed rather slow of wit), though quite well-adapted to the mountainous country of Upper Jujubia. Because of the extra weight, the expedition lasted six days, with overnight camps in the forests made more tolerable by ample supplies of Jujubian beer.

But at last, on a sunny but chilly afternoon, they reached the last line of trees before the heathery slopes that lead up towards the great snowy mountains. Most of the soldiers had never seen this sight before, and looked at each other in amazement and nervousness. The shamaness's tree house was still there as on previous expeditions of occult consultation, but it had undergone a facelift: the ancient structural beams had been refaced with fresh wood, colourful curtains had been hung in the windows, and the whole effect was prettier than before.

"It seems Bolockostra has done a makeover", observed the Speaker. His Number Three yanked the dangling rope, a little bell tinkled, the net curtains in the largest window parted, and there appeared the face of a thirty-something lady with soft wavy brown hair and a benign smile.

"Oh, we were looking for Bolockostra. Is she at home?" said the Number Three.

"Haven't you heard? Bolockostra attained Nirvana last year (Blessed be her Memory). But before she departed, she appointed me as her successor. My name is Guinevestra. How can I help you?"

The Speaker now spoke:

"Please forgive our ignorance, O Guinevestra, it takes time for intelligence to reach the lower regions. And to be frank, we were not expecting someone so *young*. Can you be the new shamaness?"

Guinevestra smiled broadly:

"I will take that as a compliment. And you can rest assured that Bolockostra and her sisterhood gave me a rigorous course of training in the shamanic arts, and after a final examination and a ten thousand word dissertation on the philosophy of shamanism, I was awarded a Mistress's degree."

The Number Two muttered something about inflation of qualifications, but the Speaker shooshed him, and said:

"O Guinevestra, we have brought you the customary cooked chicken, as a gift from the Imperial Court."

Number Three unpacked his saddle bag and produced the chicken (to which they had not forgotten to add salt and pepper, remembering their visit to Bolockostra some years before). But during the six-day journey it had passed its best before date, and there was a dubious odour. Guinevestra wrinkled up her pretty nose, and said:

"That is very sweet of you, but actually I'm vegetarian. Bolockostra may not have been completely consistent in her vegetarianism (Blessed be her Memory), but I am determined to set a better example. Besides, I don't get much exercise up here, and I don't want to lose my figure. Perhaps you would like to eat it yourselves."

That brought joy to the faces of Numbers Two and Three, but when they smelled the package, their smiles faded. They passed it to the guard of leatherclad centaurs who had been standing around, entranced by Guinevestra who seemed to have a certain something their wives and girlfriends lacked. But even they did not find the aging chicken appetizing, and they cast it into a deep ravine, upon which a rapid scurrying of nameless underground creatures was heard. Now it was time for the Speaker to raise the matter for which they had come all this way, chicken or no chicken:

"O Esteemed Guinevestra, the Imperial Council has instructed me to inquire of you concerning the unexplained disappearance of so many of the best musicians of Jujubia. What light can you throw on this grave matter? Is there, or is there not, a Bandsnatcher? And if there is, how can he, or she, or it, be apprehended or destroyed?"

Guinevestra's face became serious:

"First, I must ask you to remove your army from my lawn; such an occupation is not very polite to a harmless shamaness."

The Speaker gestured to his security detail, and thy shuffled off to a distance of a hundred yards.

"Thank you. That feels better already, doesn't it?" said Guinevestra. "Now as to the profound questions you raise, I can inform you that exists no Bandsnatcher, but there is, however, the Bandersnatch. Could there be some confusion there? May I remind you how it is written in Scripture:

Beware the Jabberwock, my son!
The jaws that bite, the claws that catch!
Beware the Jubjub bird, and shun
The frumious Bandersnatch!

Now I can assure you, you need have no fears about the Jabberwock: that species is safely extinct, due to lusty wieldings of the vorpal blades in times past by ambitious young princelings out to make a reputation for themselves (though there are those who regret the consequent loss of genetic diversity). As for the Jubjub birds, Scripture says 'beware', but I would interpret that as *be aware*, take note of their song, enjoy it, and worry only if it stops. (I believe you have had some recent experience on that matter.) Now as for the Bandersnatch ..."

"About time she got round to it," muttered Number Three, but the Speaker trod on his foot.

"... he lives up there, in the Valley of Desolation, third cave on the left," and Guinevestra pointed to a deep and dark chasm that led into the heart of the great mountains.

"And is he really frumious?" asked the Speaker.

"Well, the concept of frumiousity has been variously interpreted by the students of Scripture. One aspect of it may be the smell (*fumious*, you see), and indeed I have sometimes caught a whiffle of him when the wind blows from that direction. But another aspect of its meaning is more psychological, though the suggestion of extreme anger, as in *furious*, may be a little too obvious. However it is my belief that the Bandersnatch has been misunderstood; I think he may have unresolved mental issues."

"This is all very well, but how does it help our problem?" said the Speaker. "Is there any evidence, apart from mlinguistic coincidence, that this so-called Bandersnatch has been snatching our bands?"

"I have heard snatches of music emanating from his cave - along with the smell."

"Aha, now we are getting somewhere. So he is a music-lover - and if he has music, he must have musicians." (There was of course no technology of recorded sound in ancient Jujubia.)

"Unless he makes it himself, which I think unlikely. But, come to think of it, I'm pretty sure I heard several instruments at once."

"So some of our musicians must be still alive and playing."

"You haven't proved it is *your* musicians he has there," said Guinevestra, with serene logic befitting the holder of a Mistress's degree.

"Nevertheless, I think this is good enough evidence to take back to the Court."

The Speaker bowed and was about to take his leave, but Guinevestra spoke again:

"There is another lesson from Scripture that we have not yet learnt. It advises us to 'shun the frumious Bandersnatch', but it does not say attack him or destroy him - just *shun* him, have nothing to do to with him, give him a wide berth, see as little as possible of him."

"But what if he is kidnapping our citizens, and imprisoning them, or worse? Surely we have to act?"

"There is an interpretation of that line which I would favour - we should shun the Bandersnatch, yes, but only as long as he is frumious; if he were somehow to become less frumious, then there might be no need to shun him."

By this time the Speaker was rather losing patience with the shamaness's hermeneutics, so he quickly said:

"Thank you, O Esteemed Guinevestra, for the wealth of information and advice you have vouchsafed to us. You can rest assured that I will convey a full account to the Council."

"Whatever course of action you decide on, I would enter a plea that you treat the Bandersnatch with humanity."

"I will report that opinion to the Council, too."

So the Deputation gathered its security round itself again, and wended its weary way downhill and down dale, all the way back to the Palace. As soon as they arrived, an emergency meeting of the Council was called, allowing the Speaker only time to discard his sweaty leathers, have a cold splash, and gobble a vegetarian sandwich. He hastened up to the Council Chamber, and was amazed to find already seated there not only the Emperor but also Empress Lusciousa. This was the first time in all known history that a female had attended Council. There were some present who wondered whether the Emperor was losing his grip on reality, or at least on his unruly wife (whose serenely imperious ways had been noted, especially since the birth of her second son) - but of course no such thoughts could be breathed aloud.

After the customary prayer to the Gods of Jujubia, the Vizier turned to the Emperor, who explained the break with precedent by saying that the Empress had had intimations in a dream of the true nature of the Bandsnatcher, and wished to convey them to the Council. The Vizier only just managed to conceal a smirk, but invited Her Majesty to state her case. She smiled at everyone present, and began:

"Councillors, I know you have far more experience of state business than I. But in this time of national emergency, you need all the intelligence you can get, so I would ask you to put aside your prejudices and listen to what I have to say. This 'Bandsnatcher', as you call him, is clearly a music-lover, and I put it to you that no lover of music can be a complete monster. Moreover, I have had a dream - perhaps indeed a vision vouchsafed by the Deities of Jujubia - in which the Bandsnatcher appeared to me as a troubled individual holed up in a cave, whose only consolation in life is music. I would appeal to you to seek a psychological profile of our putative enemy, before seeking his destruction."

The Councillors glanced at each other surreptitiously with a mixture of amazement, amusement and pity. Then the Vizier cleared his throat, and said:

"Thank you, your Serene Majesty. The next item on the agenda is the report from the deputation to the shamaness."

The Speaker stood up and explained that Bolockostra had gone to Nirvana and had been replaced by Guinevestra, a younger but remarkably well-qualified shamaness, according to her own account. He then gave a summary of what she had said, explaining that the proper title of their enemy was apparently "the Bandersnatch", but omitting the details of her scriptural hermeneutics. The Councillors were duly impressed by the congruence between the Empress's dream and the shamaness's diagnosis. Lusciousa now seized the advantage of the moment, and burst out:

"Let me go and talk to him. I feel I might be able to help him achieve a better adjustment in his lifestyle."

"Dearest, we couldn't possibly take such a risk with you", said her husband, and there was a murmur of agreement around the Council.

"But it sounds like he needs *understanding*, and I think I might be able to provide it. You can give me an armed escort if you wish."

"Well ..." said the Emperor, uncertainly. The Councillors looked at each other questioningly, and there was an unspoken feeling around the table that having done her Imperial duty by producing an heir and a spare, the Empress was, well, not exactly dispensable, but perhaps a little less indispensable than before. The Vizier, experienced by long practice at discerning the sense of the meeting, now ventured to say to the Emperor:

"If we have your permission, Sire, it might be worth a try."

Judicious I did not demur. Turning to the Chief of the Defence Staff, the Vizier asked:

"Are our armed forces ready for such an expedition?"

Having received an enthusiastically affirmative answer, the Vizier summed up the feeling of the meeting that the Empress would be given a chance to negotiate with the Bandersnatch, under full escort of course, and that if that failed, the army would be authorized to take all necessary measures.

The next morning the full expeditionary force of two hundred muleback centaurs moved slowly up into the hills, followed by Empress Lusciousa in a sedan chair, carried by relays of strong-armed young farmers (agricultural production consequently went down further). Because of the elaborate arrangements required for the salubrious overnight encampment of an Empress (there was a sedan bed, and even a sedan bathroom - for which water had to be extracted from the forest streams), the journey took two weeks. When they eventually arrived at the last line of trees in Upper Jujubia, the shamaness Guinevestra, who naturally had foreknowledge of their approach, descended from her tree house, curtsied elegantly to the Empress, and invited her up for a cup of herbal tea. The two women must have hit it off, for their cup of tea took over two hours, while the army grew restive.

When the women's talk was over at last, the expeditionary force moved up into the Valley of Desolation. It was indeed a dark, fearsome place, overshadowed by some of the highest of the great mountains, with patches of dirty snow remaining through the summer, and sharp rocks that gave even the mules difficulty in placing their hooves. The conscripted young farmers of Jujubia had never been near such a place, and they felt superstitious dread. They counted the caves as the army inched its precarious way forward, and when they came within earshot of the third cave on the left, the sound of familiar music was heard - *Way-hay Jujubia!*, the most popular tune of all, arranged for dulcimer, mini-bagpipe and drum. Spirits rose. In reluctant obedience to his orders, the Commander of the Task Force beckoned the Empress's sedan chair to the front of the martial queue, and she dismounted with a flourish. He surrounded her with his ten best archers with bows at the ready, and said:

"Now, my Empress, this is the opportunity for negotiation that the Council has instructed. But if there is the least sign of trouble, you must withdraw immediately and let us sort things out."

Lusciousa smiled as only she could do, and proceeded up the slope towards the mouth of the cave. She knocked on rock, but there was no discernible sound; she looked around for a doorbell, but there was none, not even a rope. So she called out, in her most honeyed tones:

"Coo-eeee! Mr. Bandersnatch, are you at home? May I come in?"

There was a faint shuffle and a snuffle from inside. Lusciousa took that as a yes, and proceeded in her regal way up over the lip of the cave with her escort surrounding her closely. There inside sat - not a giant, only a sort of mini-giant – an obese middle-aged figure with straggly grey hair and baggy belly, in a shapeless cardigan streaked with food-stains.

On the walls of his cavern, large shelves had been carved out, and on each shelf there was parked a little band of live musicians, ready to be played at the Bandersnatch's choice. If he wanted surround sound he could make them all play together and enjoy the effect of a thousand twangling instruments. At this moment his eyes were closed, and he was listening to *Way-hay Jujubia!* with a look of transcendence on his mournful face. I have to report, however, that the smell was overpowering, for it emerged in later debriefing that he had been inducing his captive bands to play by offering them a serving of rancid yak butter, which was the only thing he had to keep them alive on.

The rest of the story can be quickly told. The Empress, courageously braving the odour, gave the Bandersnatch some intensive counselling and psychotherapy sessions over the next two weeks, with occasional visits to Guinevestra for sisterly supervision and advice. She succeeded in the end in persuading him that he was being just a little greedy in keeping the bands all to himself. He agreed to release his prisoners, and in return he was invited to come and hear the music of Jujubia whenever he wanted – provided that he cleaned up his act and promised there would be no more band-snatching, and no importing of yak butter. It took a while for the nation to recover from its trauma, and for milk production to get back to pre-war levels, but the Jujubians did live more happily for some time thereafter. However they always kept a wary eye on the Bandersnatch whenever he dropped in at a concert.

5. WHICH DOCTOR?

"Which doctor is it today?"

"Dr. Kraszka."

That's a new name ... Crashcar? ... Kafka? ... it's not auspicious.

She was a petite blonde, with a nose like a knife.

"What's your problem?"

"This thing is growing on my ear."

She called it a krasha-something-osis.

"Use this ointment."

As she signed the prescription, the fourth finger of her left hand (ringed, I noticed) tapped the desk rhythmically with its long red-painted nail, while her other claws stayed motionless. *Only a practiced musician would have such independent control. What instrument does she play? But how could she play properly, with those elongated nails?*

Two months later, I was in again.

"This thing is getting bigger."

"So I see. I'll refer you to "skins" - I mean Dermatology."

"Is it anything to worry about?"

"Oh, I don't think so. Skins will sort you out."

Her attention seemed far away. That fourth finger was drumming harder this time - and the ring had gone. Her bedside manner made me nervous about the idea of letting her anywhere near my bedroom.

Autumn came, and my krasha-something-osis dropped off of its own accord. I went in for my flu jab. Dr .Kraszka was no longer listed on the board. In the waiting room I glimpsed a lurid headline in someone's tabloid paper: "White Woman becomes Witch Doctor".

It must be her - that spooky fourth finger would surely give her great authority in the Niger Delta.

Nurse Burberry was so keen to chat she nearly forgot to give me my jab. On my way out, I asked: "What became of Dr. Kraszka?"

"Oh, she's become a special adviser in the Department of Health," said the Nurse, with pride.

It's worse - she's a spin doctor!

6. GATE ZERO

The lady guarding the entrance has such a dragon-like face I wonder if she'll breathe fire - but she just glances at my boarding card and gives me a hard look. In Security, there's a bleep when I step through the frame, and a bloke with a beer belly blocks my path. He runs his hands up my legs, and detects a hard patch in my trouser pocket. His breath is unpleasant.

"Can I see what you have there?"

I produce a pair of nail-clippers.

"Please put all metal items in the box next time, sir. We're very busy."

"Sorry to trouble you."

Now a bored-looking girl requires me to open my briefcase, and picks out the sunscreen I had optimistically slipped in at the last moment:

"Haven't you read the notices? I'll have to take this off you."

Next comes the duty-free shop, which presents an obstacle course of perfumes, sunscreen and bottled water (no doubt to profit from replacing the confiscations).

Crash

A large lady behind me has knocked over some trinket with her handbag. A voice pipes up:

"I'm afraid you'll have to pay for that."

"That's ridiculous! All this stuff is put right in our way, it's impossible not to bump into it".

"I'm sorry madam, it's company policy."

'Madam@ announces firmly: "Company policy or not, that breakage is not my fault", and turns to go. But a security guard comes up from behind the little bunch of amused onlookers:

"Madam, unless you comply with the rules of the management, you will not be allowed to board your flight."

No need to stay for the final act of that mini-drama. Let's have a look at the wines. There's a tempting special offer on the Bordeaux. But how could I carry it with me? Remember the time I was bringing back a bottle of choice Chardonnay in a plastic bag, when it swung against a metal barrier and cracked, releasing over the airport floor an expanding pool that looked more like wee than wine - as if I'd committed a miracle in reverse! I think I'll resist temptation this time.

Into the departure lounge, and check the screens. Oh hell! My flight to Lisbon is delayed by three hours. So I'll miss the reception where there would be free wine, and perhaps even an interesting female or two, though I wouldn't bet on it. What can I do for three hours, imprisoned within this ring of security? There's a sign in vibrating red neon:

GOT AN HOUR TO SPARE?
TRY GATE ZERO
THE ALTERNATIVE DESTINATION

It's probably some hole full of slot machines. I suppose I'd better try to read something by Samuel Smilesky, in whose honour the conference has been arranged. Vera, our new Head of Department, is an eager promoter of our academic reputation, and she's taken it into her head that this might be the coming thing in philosophy, so she suggested that I represent our department. And a long weekend in a three-star hotel on the coast of Portugal seemed like an attractive break from marking student essays and graduate dissertations. So to justify the jaunt, I'll find a quiet corner and address myself to the thought of the newly-famous Professor Smilesky, as published in the latest issue of *The Metaphysical Monthly*:

So far metaphysics has been obsessed with existence; the time has come to give equal treatment to non-existence. ...

Not a promising start: am I in for three days of discussion about what doesn't exist? (and without the wine reception?)

... I will classify non-being in three ways, before addressing the question of which is the most ontologically revealing categorization of unreality.

Non-being? That reminds me of Sartre's negatites. The fact that Pierre is not in the café could cause Marie to cry, if she was eagerly looking forward to a date with him. But more precisely, it would be Marie's *realization* that Pierre is not going to show up that would cause her teardrops to appear (and therein lies the mystery of psycho-physical causation). Can Smilesky do any better than Sartre, who is obscure enough himself? This threatens to be ponderous indeed, and my head's feeling heavy already.

***

Where am I? Oh, the airport. *The Metaphysical Monthly* is on the floor, and half an hour has elapsed (it often happens when I try to read philosophy after lunch). I confess I did indulge in a glass of Piesporter with my sandwich, just to start the weekend off on the right foot, as it were. That "**GATE ZERO**" sign is still blinking redly at me. I wonder what sort of "alternative" is on offer there. OK, let's check it out, I still have plenty of time to kill.

The arrow to Gate Zero is on the left of Gate 1- logically enough, I suppose. A revolving door brings me into a long featureless corridor, with a few figures disappearing round a corner in the distance. My progress is speeded by one of those long moving walkways. When I get to the corner, there's another sign:

THIS WAY TO
GATE ZERO
THE ULTIMATE DESTINATION
ALL TRAVELERS COME HERE
SOONER OR LATER

This leads to an even longer corridor. A disembodied voice says:

Congratulations on your wise choice. To assist your passage, we have arranged a speedway. Please hold on to the handrail.

I grab the rail with my free hand, and with a jerk I'm accelerated to sprinting speed. There's no such speedway going in the other direction. It feels like Alice falling down the rabbit-hole. I wonder how much time I'll need to get back, but the return route is now out of sight. The voice speaks again:

You are now approaching the Land of Zero. Please grip the rail firmly. And enjoy the rest of your life.

Taken aback by that last remark, I am suddenly decelerated, and I land in a heap; my briefcase springs open and my papers fly over the floor. A shapely young blonde with heavy makeup appears from nowhere:

"Are you all right, sir? Let me help you."

She goes down on one knee to retrieve my stuff, almost bursting out of her tight-fitting uniform as she does so - which rather distracts me from the fact that she is my examining my papers:

"What's all this? - *The Metaphysical Monthly*, Curriculum Vitae, Research Assessment Profile? You won't be needing any of this here."

"That's *my* business, don't you think?"

"Of course it is your business, sir - quite literally so. I'm just advising you that most travellers who come here soon forget about that sort of thing."

"So what *is* this place?"

"It is a place of *pleasure*, sir, where you will be *diverted*."

That sounds all right, so I pack my papers back in my case, along with the remains of my sandwich, thriftily retained for emergencies.

"Now sir", announces my angelically-smiling guide, "if you will just step up to the desk, and show me your passport. ... Thank you. Oh cool, it's one of the new biometric ones - the government likes us to keep exact records here. There you are, sir. Welcome to the Land of Zero."

"I trust there's enough time for me to get back to catch my flight?"

"Yes of course, sir. But as I was saying, most of our clients find this place so ... *different*."

This is becoming weird. Should I turn on my heel and retreat back down those long corridors? But having come this far, I may as well satisfy my curiosity: whatever foolishness may overcome others, it won't affect me.

Over the threshold of the Zero Zone, then. It's pleasantly lively, like the High Street early on a Saturday evening before the drunken youth take over.

Throbbing music and *a*nother sign in red neon:

ZERO SUM GAMES
ABANDON INHIBITION
ALL YE WHO ENTER HERE

As I suspected: dark shapes are hunched over machines with dancing lights, fast-moving pictures, and loud noise. Occasional shouts rise above the cacophony.

Clatter, clatter

A shower of coins spill onto the floor. People fight for them, yells and curses arise. It's like Plato's cave, in which the prisoners can only see images, and have no knowledge of what passes for reality outside.

Further along I come to a large establishment with a very crowded noisy bar on the ground floor. The sign reads:

THE ZERO INN
ZERO IN HERE
AND HIT YOUR TARGET

Well, I'm feeling a bit thirst by now, so let's go in for a quick one. But it takes me quite some time to push through to the bar and attract the attention of an overworked barman.

"A half of bitter, please", I shout over the din.

"What, only a half? Lose your inhibitions, guv'nor. We don't do things by halves here."

"No really, I only feel like a half."

"OK, guv, have it your own way. Would that be the moderately bitter, the extremely bitter, or the gruesomely bitter?"

I decide to show some courage after all, and plump for the latter.

"That'll be £4.50, please."

"What, a fiver for a half-pint?"

"This is no ordinary boozer", replies the barman haughtily, "this is the Zero Inn. And your gruesome bitter is no ordinary beer."

I produce a £5 note, and wait for the change, which he doesn't offer until I remind him.

"You should have gone for a pint, guv'nor - they're only £6 in the Happy Hour. We like our customers to get well started."

I've had enough of that fellow, so let's move away and find a barstool. Tentatively, I sip my half-pint. The taste is so strong it makes me cough.

"Is that the gruesome ale you're drinking?"

A husky voice in my left ear.

"Yes, but I'd no idea ...." I splutter.

"Try taking a good mouthful, and swallow it down quickly. It works better with a frontal attack."

I follow the advice, and yes, the effect is more satisfying. I feel that first lightness in the head already.

"There, that feels better, doesn't it?" says the mystery voice.

I turn to look at her. Perched on the next bar-stool is a slim redhead in a strikingly low-cut scarlet dress. I have a bit of a weakness for red hair, but hers is a bit frazzled - and isn't that a touch of greying at the roots?

"It's strong stuff", I observe, sagely.

"Oh yes, they only serve the best here."

Her eyes are lively, but bloodshot. There is a lull in the conversation: she seems to be waiting for me to take the initiative.

"Why is Gate Zero so popular?" I ask.

"Oh, lots of flights are delayed these days, and people are looking for something to do. We see the whole of life here."

"Aren't you on the way somewhere yourself?"

"We're all on the way somewhere, aren't we darling? The point is to enjoy it while we can."

Suddenly I become aware that her hand is straying up my thigh. She adds, in an even huskier voice:

"And, talking of enjoyment, how would you like to share a bottle of champagne with me? We could get an upper room."

I have led a sheltered life, and the only thing that occurs to me to reply is:

"If a half-pint of beer is £4.50, God knows what champagne will cost!" (And I assume that the lady herself would cost a lot more.)

"Oh, don't worry about the money, darling. You've only got one life - and this is the place to live it. The Inn can put it on your credit card, and you'll pay zero interest for the first month."

I come to a decision. I lift my half-pint and take a large swig, I stand up and announce: "Actually, I've a plane to catch."

"This fellow says he's got a plane to catch!" she repeats to the surrounding drinkers, who raise a chorus of guffaws, and some of them literally fall about laughing. I drain the dregs of my gruesome bitter, raise my empty glass to them, and beat a rapid retreat.

Feeling a bit unsteady, I wander further into the Land of Zero. The next sign I come upon reads:

ZERO LEGAL SERVICES
LAST WILLS & TESTAMENTS
LAST-MINUTE CHANGES
BENEFACTIONS
MALEDICTIONS
(non-zero fees)

'Maledictions'? That's a new one to me: is cursing now to be charged for (plus VAT)? I'll definitely give that establishment a miss. I stroll on beyond the bright lights, into a dark area where it goes surprisingly quiet. I have a certain feeling of instability beneath my feet - it must be that gruesome ale. There's a mysterious glimmer around the next corner, and to my astonishment I come upon a scene of moonlight reflected in a reed-fringed stream. Surely I can't have wandered right out of the airport? Let's sit down on this little stone bridge for a rest - but it's not here! I bump into a solid vertical surface instead. This whole moonlit scene is only an image projected on the wall, and the babbling brook is recorded sound!

I've had more than enough of this Zero Zone, and it must surely be time to get back to the departure lounge. I turn around, and steady myself against the wall. But the surface is moving under my fingers, and there's a tugging beneath my feet. I'm on another of those moving walkways. I try to walk quickly back the way I came, but the apparatus seems to speed up. I break into a trot, but I soon get out of breath (perhaps I should take more exercise). I can't outrun the machine, and there's nowhere to get off. I'm like the Red Queen who had to run like mad just to stay in one place. I panic, and shout for help, but nobody responds. I can't stop this insidious underfoot movement, any more than the passage of time itself.

I sit down disconsolately, and am carried into a dark tunnel. What about my mobile phone? I try to call the university, and the airline, but the message keeps coming up: NO SIGNAL. My flight will soon be departing, my vision of sunshine and wine in Portugal is fading. But perhaps all this is only a malfunction of airport technology? If I'm on a baggage conveyer, there will come a sudden emergence into light, and I should make ready to point out that I am a person, not a package, before some strong fellow in a yellow jacket throws me into the hold of a plane bound for some God-forsaken place like Mogadishu. But there's no such light at the end of this tunnel, and here's another sign to confirm I am still in the Land of Zero:

THE ZERO CHANCE SALOON
LAST SUPPERS
TAKEAWAY LAST SUPPERS

A landing-place appears where you can step off the continuously conveying belt, if you're quick. I take my chance, go into the overcrowded saloon and find one of the few remaining seats. The chap next to me is trying to order a pint of lager, but the surly waitress, wearing a pair of those party devil-horns that people put on at Hallowe'en, is saying:

"I'm sorry, sir, I've explained to you already, we only allowed to serve alcohol with meals. If you order a last supper, that includes red wine."

"Oh all right then, bring me the supper", he says, with very bad grace. The waitress looks at me and bares her teeth.

"I'll try one of those last suppers, please."

"Eat in, or takeaway?"

"Eat in, please".

During the ensuing wait I have to listen to my neighbour's complaints about anything and everything. I interrupt to ask:

"Where do you think we're going?"

"We're not going anywhere until I get a drink".

"But what's it all about?"

"It's about getting decent service."

No point in seeking enlightenment from him. When the 'last supper' comes, it consists of a slice of soggy white bread, a phial of reddish liquid, and in between there's a bowl of steaming featureless substance that must have been transubstantiated in a microwave. My neighbour knocks back the liquid, and leaves without touching the food. I try all three offerings, but none of them are at all palatable.

Loud threatening voices

I look round, and see armed guards ordering all customers who have finished their suppers to leave.

I step onto the conveyer belt again, and we are delivered onwards into the tunnel. Doors occasionally open from the side, and small groups of people are ushered onto the moving surface. Many of them are black or brown. Most come quietly, but some put up a fight. I hear screams, and the belt brings me towards a platform on which a young black woman is struggling with a heavy bloke. Anger rises inside me, and I jump on beside them:

"What do you think you're doing, hitting a woman like that?"

"Mind your own business, mate, or I'll duff you one too."

A small black boy is crying beside us, and I put an arm round him. A large fist clunks into my face, my glasses fall and shatter, and the three of us are brusquely shoved onto the ever-moving belt, where we sit in a sullen heap.

"Where are you from?" I eventually ask.

"Birmingham. I was born there, but they're deporting us."

Her Brummie accent is impeccable.

"Oh dear", is my pathetic reaction.

After a while, I ask the boy his name.

"Sebastian."

"Hullo, Sebastian."

"Hi", he squeaks shyly.

I can't think of anything more to say in these extraordinary circumstances, and we are propelled onwards in silence. Now there looms up one more circular sign:

ZERO CREED
INTER-FAITH CHAPEL
PAUSE FOR THOUGHT
BEFORE YOU DEPART

There's the usual landing-stage, so I exclaim "Time out!" and the three of us stumble off. I have glanced into airport chapels before, but I've never seen one so full. In front is a white wall on which in no particular order are inscribed a star of David, a cross, a crescent, a mini-Buddha, a Krishna, and a variety of other hieroglyphics. People around us are praying, meditating, or just sitting and maybe thinking. I recognize my bad-tempered neighbour from the Zero Chance Saloon, now on his knees muttering:

"Oh God! ... I've forgotten about you until now ... I'll do anything ... if only ..."

Some Muslims are prostrating themselves in what they must have guessed is the direction of Mecca. A woman is meditating in lotus position with a beatific smile on her face. There is complete silence, and it has a strangely intense effect. Most people seem to become calmer than when they came in. But the place is getting overcrowded and stuffy, and we can hardly stay forever. My two companions follow me out, and there is no option but to step back onto that ever-moving black belt. It's very full now: people of all shapes and sizes, old and young, obese and slim, black and white, brown and yellow, cool and not-so-cool, all being transported inexorably forward. A disembodied voice of sickly-sweet tone now announces:

Dear travellers, you are now approaching the last stage of your earthly journey. You are privileged to be amongst the first to explore cosmic space. We know you started out with a different destination in mind, but we feel sure that you will recognize the distinction that has been conferred on you. In fact, we have a message for you from the Prime Minister himself.

An enlarged, inanely grinning face of our Great Leader is projected on the tunnel wall, and it travels alongside us with his recorded voice:

Hello travellers. I just wanted to say how much I appreciate what you are doing for our country. As you know, our island is getting overpopulated, we have an energy shortage, and a looming pensions crisis. I would like you to know that I believe very sincerely that great benefit will accrue from your journey - for those who remain behind. I also want to congratulate the Management of Gate Zero on the success of this, our latest public-private initiative. Thank you, and goodbye.

At this, some people try to run backwards against the motion of the belt. But even the most athletic - a muscly young black man - can only manage to stay in one place for a few seconds by sprinting. Sebastian tries to imitate him, but his Mum calls him back, and he runs forwards again and bumps into us at speed. We are moved steadily forwards together. Then he suddenly squeals:

"Ma, I'm hungry!"

She lifts her hands mournfully to indicate that she has nothing to give him. I remember my leftover half-sandwich, so I open my briefcase and offer him the dubious delicacy. His eyes light up, his mum smiles for the first time, and they say simultaneously:

"Thank you."

Now we get one more announcement from our guardian angel:

Now, dear travellers, we need to mention a practical point. There are restrictions of space in cosmic travel, so we invite you to drop your cabin baggage through the holes provided. You can rest assured that the materials will be recycled in an environmentally-friendly way for the use of others.
The management team of Gate Zero would like to take this opportunity of wishing you a happy trip, even if you will never be tripping with us again.

Some people obediently drop off their bags, but others don't. I recognize "Madam" from the duty-free shop (which now seems a long time ago) grimly clutching on to her capacious handbag. What about my briefcase? I may as well hang onto it - perhaps in cosmic space there will be time to study those scholarly papers. But on second thoughts, I reckon non-existence itself would be preferable to an eternity of reading Professor Smilesky on non-existence. I drop my case through the last available hole, and proceed towards my destiny without academic encumbrances. (So that cheeky young blonde was right after all.)

As Sebastian enjoys the remains of my sandwich, our forward movement accelerates, and the tunnel turns upwards. A circular shape comes into view, a glossy black hole with tiny particles whirling into it - a big round Zero, filled with non-existence. As the people in front of us approach it, their bodies are momentarily outlined against the intense blackness, then abruptly disappear. I'm holding one hand of my new-found friend while his Mum holds the other, there comes a whooshing sound, and ...

7. A LIFT TO THE SPIRIT

'You're looking a bit down in the mouth - what's wrong, Janice?'

Janice stamped Daisie's library card for the latest romantic blockbuster, and sighed:

'Oh, nothing in particular.'

'How's Laura doing?'

'She's settled well into secondary school, and now she's always out with her new friends.'

'And Aidan?'

'Oh, his life revolves around football and computer games. But they both got quite good reports last term.'

'So why the sad face?'

'Do I look sad? … Well, I don't know, maybe something seems to be missing, now that the kids are more independent. We don't do things as a family any more.'

'How's John?'

'He's under pressure to develop new marketing plans, and he often has to bring work home. Then he nods off in front of the TV.'

'He's lucky to have a job at all. So many people are being let go these days.'

'Yes, you're right, of course.'

Janice didn't confess to Daisie that she was finding John a bit boring too. When the family did things together everyone had fun, but now what was the point of her life apart from the daily round of domesticity and librarianship? She had more time to herself, but she didn't know what to do with it. When she lay awake, with John already snoring, she reflected that she had gone through the day on automatic pilot, and didn't quite know where she had landed.

But when Daisie returned her blockbuster next week she smiled and presented Janice with a poster for the notice-board announcing: "The New Spirit".

'What's that?' asked Janice.

'Haven't you heard about it? It's this new movement that's going all round the country. I went to a meeting with my friend Val, and His Witness spoke directly to our hearts.'

'His Witness?'

'That's what they call the leader. You should hear him speak, he's really impressive. He helps people "find the Spirit". Why don't you come to the next meeting? It might be just what you need, Janice!'

'Oh, it doesn't sound like my sort of thing at all.'

'Well, you'll never know unless you try.'

Thus it was that, not having darkened the door of a church since her marriage (apart from four funerals and a wedding), Janice met Daisie outside the local church hall one rainy evening. Inside were about twenty women, one elderly gent with a long beard, and a rather smelly dachshund. Amidst a hushed but expectant buzz, Janice shyly sat down beside Daisie on a rickety chair in the back row. Presently a young man in a sharply-cut business suit appeared on stage and held up his hands to the ceiling. After a rather prolonged silence, he pronounced solemnly:

'May the Spirit be with us tonight.'

There was another long pause, during which Janice nervously wondered what was going to happen. Then he delivered a little speech in a mid-Atlantic accent:

'Welcome to the first meeting of the New Spirit in this town, and a special welcome to the newcomers amongst you. You know, folks, thousands more have been joining our Movement in recent weeks. They have been finding what was missing in their lives. They have experienced the Spirit, and they have brought others to experience it too. Tonight we are privileged to have a visitation from our Leader in the Spirit. Not every town is so fortunate as to be graced with the presence of His Witness himself. Please stand, and bow your heads.'

With a shuffle of chairs, the little congregation got to their feet. Janice joined in the head-bowing, but sneaked a look as two more young men carried in a large red swivel chair, behind which a tall figure in a white flowing robe strode in majestically, and occupied his portable throne. He raised the microphone to his lips, and his deep voice resounded round the room:

'The Spirit is with us.'

Everyone sat down, and the Leader's gaze panned slowly towards each person in turn, in complete silence. Most people met his eyes for a moment, then dropped theirs. Janice got apprehensive, and when those penetrating dark eyes stared into hers, she shifted on her feet, her chair squeaked, and the dachshund barked twice. She felt a tremendous blush come over her face, and quickly bowed her head.

She couldn't remember much of the rest of the meeting. His Witness's voice was as hypnotic as his gaze. He discoursed at length about "the New Spirit", and Janice felt that he was offering her just what she had been vaguely wishing for. She did recall, though, that towards the end he said that if you really want to experience the New

Spirit in your life, you have to be prepared to give something of yourself to the Movement. After His Witness finished his oration, the first young man then explained how the Movement needed funds to bring the Spirit to more and more people up and down this land. He announced a silent collection, and a pristine white bowl was passed down Janice's row. In her mood of spiritual uplift, she felt ready to contribute, but when she opened her handbag she found she had nothing less than a £20 note - which was four times the figure she first thought of. But then she noticed that other people - even Daisie, who was she knew was not well off - were producing tenners and twenties, so she felt obliged to drop hers in too.

Janice walked home with a lightness in her head that felt rather like those few occasions when she could remember getting pleasantly tipsy. At home she found John poring over his spreadsheets:

'Do you know, John, I've just experienced the New Spirit.'

'What? You are a bit pink in the face. What sort of spirit was that? Have you been drinking?'

'Don't be so literal. I told you I was going to the New Spirit meeting with Daisie.'

'So what happened?'

'His Witness filled me with the Spirit, and I feel like a new person.'

'His Witness? What sort of silly title is that?'

'That's what they call him. He's so impressive, he made me feel completely different.'

'His Witless, more likely. You seem to have lost *your* wits.'

'Oh, you don't understand. It's something you have to *feel*.'

John noticed she had got pinker still and there were tears in her eyes, so he changed tack:

'Well, if it's so important to you …'

'Yes, it is. I wish you'd come to the next meeting.'

'Oh, dear, do I have to?'

'You don't have to, but I'd love it if you did.'

He decided there was no answer to that, and kept silent.

'Please, John, let's try something new, we've got stuck in a rut lately.'

'Well, if we must.'

The next meeting of the New Spirit consisted of ten people squashed into someone's front room a few streets away. Janice and John were received with embarrassingly effusive welcomes, and were solemnly informed that His Witness was present "not in body, but in Spirit". An immaculately-presented redhead encouraged each person to testify to the New Spirit in their life. They all said much the same thing - about meaningfulness, uplift, sacrifice, and devotion to His Witness. Janice felt very self-conscious in John's presence, but when her turn came she managed a few words:

'Yes, since I first heard His Witness, I have felt a New Spirit in my life. It's hard to describe, it's something you just have to feel.'

When attention turned to John, he would only say:

'I'm here to listen, not to talk.'

After their hostess had plied them with tea and cakes, the business-suited lady announced:

'Before we go out infused with the New Spirit, let us make our commitment to this great Movement of ours, in the spirit of sacrifice which His Witness has commended. I have here the Solemn Covenants which He has individually prepared for you. When you have made your covenant, you will receive your own personalized edition of the Spirit Box, for you to enshrine in your homes and in your hearts.'

So saying, she reverently unveiled a small perspex pyramid containing a white ball inscribed with mysterious hieroglyphics. John emitted an involuntary snigger, which he tried to cover with a cough. Janice caught his eye, and began coughing too. Their hostess plied them with glasses of water. When order was restored, covenant forms were passed around. John looked at the small print and noted the Direct Debit for unspecified amounts, so he politely resisted the persistent pressure to sign up there and then. Janice whispered:

'Shouldn't we make a commitment?'

He whispered back:

'We can take the form home with us, and think about it.'

As they walked home in pensive silence, they passed the church nearest their house, where there was a board displaying a verse from *Galatians*: "The fruit of the Spirit is love, joy, peace, patience, kindness, goodness, fidelity, gentleness, and self-control".

John remarked quietly: 'As you know, I'm not a religious person, but that sounds a better sort of Spirit to me.'

Janice remained silent for a few moments. Then she burst into tears, and put her arms around his neck in a way she hadn't done for years.

8. NEMATODE ISLAND

Josie had been rather moody that afternoon, until we landed on the uninhabited islet. She was an only child who lived in the next street from us, and when her mum heard that I was taking Jennie and Tom on a boat trip that Saturday she asked if Josie could be included too. Josie was a bit older than our two, just on the cusp of adolescence, often with a bored and superior look on her face, but I didn't see that as too much of a problem, so I readily agreed to let her join us.

The mail-boat set off up the loch in glorious sunshine dancing off the choppy water, but after a while the clouds came over and we began to feel chilly in the wind. Josie twisted her red hair in her hands, and said "This is no fun". Then I had what I thought was a brilliant idea to make our outing more interesting: I asked the skipper if he would drop us off on the lonely island just coming up, about half-way to the remote settlement at the head of the loch (one of the very few places in Britain that you can only get to by boat). The skipper said, morosely, "No one ever goes *there*", but he agreed to let us off and pick us up again on his way back, around sunset in a couple of hours' time.

Released from the stiffness of sitting in the small boat, Josie led the way and skipped straight into the clump of dark thorn bushes and skeletal trees at the centre of the island. When we caught up with her in the small clearing within, Tom stumbled over the crumbling remains of a wall, and yelped. I helped him wipe the blood off his knee.

Josie spoke first: "I wonder if anyone ever lived here?"

"I doubt it, this is a small island", I said, "there's nothing to eat."

"Maybe fish", said Tom, brightly.

"I wouldn't like to eat nothing but fish", said Jennie.

"With no chips", added Josie.

That prompted me to get out our jam sandwiches out of my backpack, and we all greedily tucked in. As we munched, Tom, who always had an inquiring mind, suddenly asked:

"Why are there trees on the island but none on the land all round?"

I gave the biologically correct answer: "It's because bushes and trees were the original vegetation covering most of Scotland, before there were humans and their animals. The sheep nibble everything except heather, but they can't get to islands. So, if you think about it, we're in a remnant of the prehistoric wildwood!"

"But these stones are in a square, they look like the remains of a house", said Josie.

"Maybe it was a summer cottage for fishermen, or a little shrine", I suggested. Then it occurred to me to add: "It might have been a place for pagan rituals."

"What's pagan?" asked Jennie.

"Oh, it means the kind of religion people had in ancient times, before Christianity", I explained, "they worshipped nature, and believed in elves and fairies and magical stuff like that."

I began to be conscious of an unnameable smell around us, and a sudden gust of wind whistled round our necks and rattled some dead branches above us.

"This place is creepy", Jennie wailed, and put her little hand in mine.

I felt it was a bit eldritch myself, but judged it better not to say so, because I would have to explain the meaning of the word to the kids, and it might have made them nervous. I decided we'd better have an action plan:

"Let's explore the whole island. I'll go to the north; Jennie, you look at the east side over there; Tommy to the west; and Josie, you're the biggest, you can run down south to the far end. See what you can find, then come back here and we'll say what we've observed."

I couldn't see any harm in that. The island was only a few hundred yards long after all, and I could see every corner of it from where we were.

***

When we met up again in the central space among the prickly bushes, Tommy reported: "I saw a dead crow floating belly-up, with its beak pointing in the air."

"Maybe it died of fright", said Josie, with a scowl.

"Perhaps it just got old", I suggested.

Meanwhile Jennie was jumping up and down to exclaim: "I found a fairy ring in the grass over there. Mum was reading to me about them last night in my new book."

"Those dark circles in the sward are caused by fungi puffing out their spores", I scientifically explained - but Jennie's face fell.

From my own investigation I reported:

"Guess what I found at the north end - a little shingly beach, and on it were two perfect circles of pebbles."

"Maybe the fairies are using stones these days", Tom suggested, with one of his most mischievous grins.

Jennie made a rude noise at him, and Josie snorted and tossed her mane of red hair. I said, pacifically:

"It's what they call land art - someone's been here before us."

But it was Josie who discovered the worms. I knew that she loved to get hands-on with creatures of all kinds, and she had brought back from her expedition to the southern tip of our mysterious island a couple of slender unsegmented cylinders (*nematodes*, as I identified them later, after the events of that day). They were very thin, and didn't wriggle, but they had a rather peculiar odour - whether pleasant or unpleasant I couldn't quite decide.

"Yuk", squealed Jennie, "how could you pick those things up?"

Josie threw one at her, and she screamed, loud enough to make us all jump. But Tom said:

"Hey, did you see it light up?"

Josie tossed the other one at *him* - and yes, it did become luminescent as it flew through the air. It slipped through his hands, and when he bent to pick it up he exclaimed:

"Wow! There are hundreds of them!"

Among those mossy stones he had disturbed earlier there was a seething mass of nematodes.

"Let's see if they *all* light up", Tom shouted, and he started throwing the worms about in all directions. They made dancing patterns of light against the overhanging bushes and the darkening loch. Josie kept chucking them back at him, and somehow I couldn't resist trying my hand at the worm-tossing too. They weren't slimy, and their smell seemed to dissipate as their candlepower increased.

After a while even little Jennie joined in the fun, and her whoops of glee mingled with Josie's increasingly manic cackles of laughter.

The four of us started to cavort around those ancient stones, amid our flickering threads of airy light. The surrounding hills themselves seemed to sway with us, and after a while I even fancied I heard faint music carried on the freshening breeze. Neither we nor our fairy-lights seemed to run out of energy, it felt as if we could go on for ever. After a while it seemed as if our feet were no longer touching the ground, and we experienced a strange lightness of being. But there was also a certain loss of control as we lost contact with the earth. All I can remember is that the whirling lights got even brighter and more beautiful as the background of loch and mountains went black.

***

Next thing I knew, there was a searchlight approaching up the loch, the roar of a speedboat, then two Scottish policemen with their black-and-white chequered caps landed on the pitch-dark island, followed by another figure I could hardly see.

"Where on earth were you?" they said. "The skipper couldn't see you on the island, and now it's nearly midnight."

I felt faint, and I struggled to get some words out:

"Er … I seem to remember … we were dancing with the worms."

"Dancing with worms? What kind of talk is that?"

I could formulate no reply. Jennie and Tom were clinging to me, shivering in the cold wind. Then a voice I recognized as Josie's dad shouted desperately:

"Where's Josie?"

and I realized with a chill to my heart that she was not with us.

***

I'll spare you the details of the aftermath - the searches, the recriminations, the police interviews, the court case. Every inch of our little island was pored over by white-coated agents of the law, but no trace of Josie was found and no adolescent body was ever washed up on the desolate shores of that loch, which afterwards seemed so sinister to us. At one point it seemed I might be charged with murder, but it was reduced to negligence, and my lawyer got me off on a technicality.

I even had some trouble getting my wife to believe my story, though I think I just about managed to convince her in the end. But Josie's parents never spoke to us again – understandably, I suppose - and we all moved away from the West Highlands. Tom and Jennie have grown up happily enough - he's at university now, and she'll go next year - and though we can never forget our night of dancing with the nematodes, we somehow find it comforting to think that Josie went off with the fairies.

9. TIME TRAIN

Have you ever heard of a train being fifty years early? My unexpected voyage through the zones of time began as a perfectly ordinary trip from Edinburgh to Leuchars, from where I would use my bus pass for the last six miles to St.Andrews. I got to Platform 18 in Waverley Station in good time, and chose a window seat on what would be the seaward side.

A shaven-headed bloke with a tattoo of a half-naked woman on his biceps took the seat opposite me. He uttered a friendly "Hiya", and opened today's *Sun*, displaying for my delectation the blazing headline: PAST SINS OF GAY VICAR. Then a well-dressed lady sat down beside me and immediately immersed herself in a book. I caught a glimpse of the title - *Remembrance of Things Past,* volume 6, by Marcel Proust - and was duly impressed (you don't see many of *them* these days). Diagonally across the rather stained table there appeared a sharp-suited young fellow with jet-black hair, worn rather long for a businessman, who took out his laptop and mobile as soon as we were through the Edinburgh tunnels and started discussing in a loud voice we couldn't help overhearing the agenda of an upcoming meeting of sales representatives.

As we trundled over the Forth Bridge, I looked down at that mournful rocky islet encrusted with bird-stained ruins and now inhabited only by seagulls, and I reflected on the times when it would have been bristling with artillery to discourage the Spanish, Dutch, French, or German navies from any closer acquaintance with Scottish shores. Evidence from bygone centuries was only a few feet below us, but nowadays invasion might take the form of corporate takeovers or cyber-warfare. The tableful of young men wearing football scarves across the aisle were now cracking open the second round from their large box of lager cans, and the noise level rose. I had taken out my copy of Heidegger's *Being and Time*, which I thought I would dip into in preparation for the afternoon seminar by a visiting German philosopher, but with all the distractions around me I found my mind just would not stay with that extremely ponderous prose.

So I daydreamed the time away, enjoying those familiar views of the varying Fife coast, with its stretches of sand, leafy woodland, half-abandoned little harbours, ship-breaking yards, and rocky cliffs and holiday homes in the bit towards Kirkcaldy, which was the first stop on this fast service. But after some passengers disembarked there, the train sat in the station for an unusually long time. A silence fell, on the lager drinkers, then broken by the bald head opposite:

'Oh-oh. Here we go.'

Then came the announcement:

Scotrail apologize for the delay, which is caused by the train in front running slow. We hope to have you moving again shortly.

'Typical', said the tattoo, and I nodded agreement.

After another ten minutes we started again with a jerk, and moved forward slowly. The lager-lads opened their third can (or was it their fourth?), their voices rose yet louder, and the young businessman started another phone conversation which was more about football than salesmanship. But before we got to Markinch we ground to a halt again, somewhere in the middle of the country this time.

'What's wrong now?' said the bloke opposite.

It occurred to me that I might miss the seminar on Heidegger, but I confess I did not feel much regret. The lady beside me was still deeply immersed in Proust's memories of his past, and seemed oblivious of the present. Through the window I gazed on a siding with rusty rails, decaying wooden sleepers, and baby trees growing up between them. More relics of the past, I thought - why do they leave those ancient sidings to rot away slowly? If they're not using them, why don't they clear them away? Maybe they can't afford to? Or do they leave them there just in case they might come in useful in an emergency? Well, it seemed there was some sort of emergency on now, for after another long wait, the tannoy announced:

Ladies and gentlemen, Scotrail regret to inform you that the train in front of us has broken down, and the line is blocked. Please be patient while we try to arrange an alternative route.

The lady beside me put down her Proust, and said:

'Alternative route? I know of no other line from here. What can they be talking about?'

'Perhaps they mean buses', said the businessman.

'But we're stuck in the middle of nowhere. They couldn't get buses across these muddy fields', said he of the shaven head.

'Maybe we'll have to walk along the line', I suggested.

'How thrilling!' said the literary lady.

Our musings were interrupted as the train suddenly moved *backwards*, stopped, then forwards again. There was a repeated sound like 'snap-brush ... crackle-swish', and seeing no track to my right this time, I realized that we had been diverted onto the disused siding I had just been contemplating, and the train was breaking off those little trees as we went over them. I have sometimes fantasized about those mysterious branch lines that disappear round a corner into the woods, imagining a children's story with some quite extraordinary destination at the end of the line. But now my fantasy seemed to be coming true, for we did not bump into buffers but proceeded gently down such a branch line (through the woods indeed), with gentle cracklings and swishings that did not seem to impede our progress.

'Where on earth are we going? I don't recognize this line', said my neighbour, with some alarm in her voice.

'It must be an old industrial branch. I bet we end up in a disused linoleum factory. There's lots of them around Kirkcaldy', said the bloke opposite.

'Hardly the destination we had in mind,' she responded.

'At least they could get buses there.'

'That'll delay us by hours, and I've got a meeting to make,' said the businessman impatiently.

'Wasn't there once a loop line through the East Neuk of Fife, connecting all the fishing villages and going right round to St.Andrews?' I offered, as a clumsy attempt at humour.

'Yes, but that was closed many years ago, and the track has been dismantled long since', replied the sharp suit, with an air of superior knowledge.

At that, our train suddenly accelerated, and entered a tunnel where everything went black. When we came out, there was a change in its rhythm, a clacketty-clack that hadn't been there before. Clouds of white smoke were drifting past the window, and there was a puffing sound. It seemed we were now being pulled by a steam-engine - an extinct species on regular services. A window was open, and some of the smoke blew into my face. I blinked, my eyes watered, and I had to get a tissue out to wipe them. When I opened my eyes again, the shaven head with tattoos had disappeared, and there instead was an elderly gentleman in a three-piece tweed suit, a watch chain, and half-moon glasses. He unfolded an old-style full-size copy of *The Daily Mail*, and on the front page was the headline: BRITISH TROOPS GRAB SUEZ. But that was in 1956! I thought I must be dreaming. Yet the smoke seemed very real, as did the irritation it caused in my eyes and throat.

The businessman hadn't changed in age, but he was now in a pinstripe suit of old-fashioned cut, with a leather briefcase instead of a laptop and mobile, and with short hair brylcreemed back. The lads across the aisle retained their football scarves, but they now wore their hair in quiffs that had also benefited from the brylcreem. It was like watching one of those black-and-white film clips of the teddy boys of the 1950s. They were still making a lot of noise, though their alcohol had vanished. But now the pinstripe leaned over to them, and said:

'I say, old chaps, would you mind keeping the noise down a bit? Some of us have got work to do.'

The nearest one said: 'Certainly, sir', and the next one said 'Sorry'.

And thereafter they did indeed keep their conversation to average level - a result which I regarded as truly miraculous. This alone was enough to make me think we had slipped into the past, when manners were supposed to have been better. However the tweedy gent now took out his pipe, got it lit on the third try, and proceeded, without so much as a "By your leave", to puff out clouds of bluish smoke, most of which seemed to waft in my direction. I started to cough, and I realized that there was cigarette smoke in the mix too, from elsewhere in the carriage. I always hated smoke in confined places, but in this carriage at this untimely time it was unavoidable. And somehow the age and bulk of his tweediness intimidated me from registering any complaint.

The train now slowed down, passing a pair of horses pulling a plough. The ploughman gave us a friendly wave, and we squeaked to a halt. The platform signs said: CRAIL - which is the fishing village at the corner of the East Neuk, the farthest end of the peninsula that used to be known as the Kingdom of Fife. Yes, once upon a time there was a railway station here, and if you look carefully you can see traces of the embankment where the track used to run, but within living memory the place has been turned into a garden centre. Yet here we were, with clouds of steam blowing about and a uniformed porter politely assisting a holidaying family to climb on board with their battered leather suitcases, shrimping nets, and old-fashioned loopy tennis racquets. The whistle sounded, the engine puffed, and we rounded the bend to proceed north-westwards towards St.Andrews.

We picked up speed and passed between the walls of a cutting, and for a few seconds the carriage went dark. When we came out into sunlight again, I was wearing short trousers and a sleeveless pullover, and I seemed to have shrunk in size. I found in my hand a currant scone, well plastered with butter and raspberry jam. I bit into it, of course - what else do you do with such a delicacy? It was quite delicious, and suddenly I remembered my dear old Gran: only *she* made scones quite like that - her "special recipe" she used to say. And then the hairs on the back of my neck rose, for I had the overwhelming feeling that she was sitting right beside me. And there to my left, instead of that intellectual lady who had embarked at Edinburgh, was a faded flowery dress that I recognized from way back in my boyhood. I looked up into that familiar smiling face framed by wispy white hair, I choked on my mouthful of scone, and began to splutter.

'There, there, don't gobble so quickly', she said, with that penetrating voice that I hadn't heard for so many years. I got my mouth back into order, but my emotions were out of control:

'Gran, how did *you* get here? It's been years since I saw you.'

My eyes had already been well-watered by the smoke, but now I burst into tears.

'What are you talking about? And why are you crying, you funny fellow? You're supposed to be a big boy now.'

I remembered that Gran could be quite sharp, as well as kindly.

'Gran, I thought I'd never see you again.'

'What's got into you today? We're going for a nice trip to St.Andrews, the weather is beautiful, you've got your jammy scone, and you start blubbing!'

I pulled myself together as best I could, and attempted a rational conversation:

'How's Grandad?'

'What a question! Don't you remember? He passed away last year. He'll be up there in heaven, arguing with the angels that they shouldn't really exist.'

I remembered that my grandfather had a reputation for atheism.

'Do atheists get to heaven?'

'The good ones do', said Gran, with great certainty.

But that was the last I heard from my Gran - though it was a great line by which to remember her brief second coming - for our train now entered a tunnel, another thing that shouldn't really exist on the flat stretch between Crail and St.Andrews. Everything went black and the noise was extreme, but the smoke disappeared. When we emerged, the vision had vanished like a dream: everyone in the carriage was back to how we were when we started, including myself, relieved to be out of the short trousers, but rather disappointed to have been brought back so soon to what passes for normal.

I now recognized the scene you see after leaving Cupar station - the Eden river winding around those peculiar lumpy fields. By some magic we were now back on the main line, and with diesel power again. I would have to get off at Leuchars and wait for the bus after all (the branch line to St.Andrews having been closed in 1969). I had begun to fantasize about arriving at the defunct station between those high stone walls (now a car park), where I would be able to step into the lost world of 1950s St.Andrews with its ancient but tiny university, red-gowned students, eccentric professors, and plus-foured golfers. But now the tannoy announced:

Scotrail would like to apologize for your train getting set back some years, but with the help of our latest timeline technology we have been able to make up the lost time. We thank you for your patience, and we hope you will find the time to travel with Scotrail again.

It occurred to me that I had been vouchsafed an experience of time that was more profound than anything in Heidegger, perhaps even rivalling Proust (I must really get around to reading him some time, when I have a year or two free). But my musings were interrupted by that familiar nannying voice:

We are approaching Leuchars. If you are leaving the train, please ensure that you take all your personal belongings with you. But, dear passengers through time, if there any personal qualities *that you would rather be without, please feel free to leave them behind.*

10. A TASTE OF TERROR

It's nearly time to go, but I want to hear what the Muslim philosopher has to say. And I fancy one more slice of toast with this curry-flavoured marmalade that Jimmy discovered.

"Are we winning the war on terror?"

"It's not a war. There aren't two states fighting each other, there can never be a surrender, or a peace treaty."

"But are we any nearer stopping terrorism?"

"No, quite the reverse. Many more Muslims around the world have been motivated to join jihadist groups."

Yeah, we told you so back in 2003. When Jimmy and I skived off school to join the march, our placard said:

THIS WAR WILL PROVOKE MORE TERRORISM THAN IT PREVENTS.

Our classmates sat down in the street with us then, but now they've given up activism. They're either drinking hard or working hard on their IT, hoping for well-paid jobs. But we've kept the faith - and here's the Today programme agreeing with us.

"But there haven't been any more deaths from terrorism in Britain since 7/7."

"Well, the security services can't be lucky every time. There could be an operation this very day."

"What? Do you know something we don't? Shouldn't you be telling the police?"

"It's only my intuition. I wouldn't expect the police to listen to it."

"Luke, it's 8.20, you'll be late."

"OK, Mum, I'm off."

No time to clean my teeth, I'll have to live with the hot taste of that marmalade. Out into a typical November morning in Glasgow, with a grey lid over the sky and that West of Scotland mizzle that hangs in the air and wets your hair in minutes. Better jog to the station to make up time. But the piles of leaves are slimy …

"Ouch!!"

"Are you all right there?"

It's Mrs.McAllister cleaning her step. The older wifies round here try to maintain traditional standards of Scottish cleanliness.

"Have you hurt yourself?"

"No, I just slipped up."

God, there's a bedraggled bird under my feet. It's going for the greasy remains of a bag of chips - a favourite feast of the urban rook. It even seems to be offering me one. No thanks, mate, have it all yourself.

"You need to watch your step on a driech day like this. And look at your trews! What a shame - you'd better go home and change."

"No time for that, I'm late already."

On Western Avenue, the traffic is spraying more wetness into the air. Horns blare as I weave across between the cars. But why the road rage? I'm not delaying them. Down into the underground at

Kelvinbridge. There's a train coming, better run for it. But these two obese youths are waddling right in my way.

"Oh shit."

The larger one leers into my face through a half-chewed burger, dripping cheese.

"What are you shitting about?"

Better back off. It's going to be one of those days. The College is so strict about punctuality, I may have the dubious pleasure of an interview with Dr. Catriona Campbell, the Depute Rector who's so obsessive about 'standards proper to the College'. Here's the next train, full to bursting. I'll just have to squeeze myself into the mass of bodies. My specs are covered in Glaswegian drizzle, and it's a struggle to extract a tissue from my pocket. Wow! What a view! The latest fashion is for these ingeniously-designed bras ('masterpieces of micro-engineering', say the advertisements) which offer teasing glimpses of boobs from several angles. Jimmy put its down to the capitalist drive for profits. His family go back to the days of Red Clydeside, and are still proud to call themselves socialists. I'm surprised he tolerates an Englishman like me.

It's hard to ignore these fleshy temptations thrust right under my nose. And I can't avoid bumping into them when the train lurches. I'm getting hot, my glasses are steaming up again. Another awkward wipe. Her face is heavily made-up, and rather hard-looking. And wasn't that a hostile glance, when our eyes momentarily met? Not so attractive after all. The Muslims tell women to cover themselves, but can't there be a happy medium between this commercially-encouraged striptease and the black burka?

Let's try to concentrate on the business of the day. There'll be the usual large dose of IT, our Strathclyde-Microsoft College being one of the new academies specializing in what's thought relevant to economic growth. I think I've done enough to get by in IT, but what

I'm looking forward to is History. Dr. McNabb (known to us all as "the Nab") will be continuing our module on the Middle East. Last time he was explaining how the Navy's need for oil led the British to carve the new state of Iraq out of the corpse of the Ottoman Empire after the First World War. ... God, it's oppressive in here. I think I'll just shut my eyes until Argyle Street.

**

The railway line leads across a flat, broiling-hot desert - but at one point the rails stop, though sleepers continue. From over the horizon there puffs a steam engine, slowly pulling a motley collection of bullet-scarred carriages and vans. As it nears the end of the rails, it squeaks to a halt. Soldiers in khaki uniform jump out and set up firing positions. Swarthy workmen bring heavy tools, and start lifting rails from behind the train, carrying them forward, and resetting them to extend the track in front. It is slow work in the heat of the sun, and by this laborious process the train can travel only a few miles per day.

**

I know where that image comes from - on the Nab's recommendation, I was reading last night how the British installed a puppet government in Iraq in the 1920s, but there was violent opposition from insurgents. Their favoured target of attack was the railways, the main means of communication at the time, and they took to lifting track. One notorious train, celebrated in railway lore as the "Diwaniya Special", took eleven days to complete a journey of sixty miles by relaying track in front of itself. That beats all British records for lateness!

Another bump into this buxom secretary, or whoever she is. "Sorry".

We're nearly at Buchanan Street station. What's that fizzing sound? There's a tingle in my nose, too. Could it be one of those new erotic perfumes? ... But now there's a strange taste in my mouth, and I feel dizzy. The train is braking, people are screaming and falling over. Suddenly I'm right on top of her, with my head cushioned between those bulging breasts.

"Geroffme!"

"Sorry, I can't help it".

"What's that smell?"

Is it the perfume, the rotting leaves, or the curry-flavoured marmalade? Oof! My breath is pumped out as someone collapses on top of me, and now my face is pushed over hers. Her body may be immobilized, but her head isn't, and she's applying her lips to mine. My first kiss, actually - but the taste of her thick lipstick combined with whatever's in my mouth is revolting. I feel paralyzed, and I can't get away from her grip. I'm trapped in a nightmarish, bad-tasting, and involuntary clinch.

***

Where am I? In bed in a silent white room. I feel weak all over, but with an effort I can sit up. These aren't my pyjamas, they're a sickly shade of yellowish-green. Straight through the window is a gothic spire of grime-darkened stonework - I know it, it's the Cathedral of St.Mungo! I must be in the Royal Infirmary, that pile of modern concrete and glass, built so conveniently beside the graveyard as Jimmy remarked. This was once the hub of Glasgow, but when the medieval town expanded into an industrial metropolis, the centre moved down nearer the Clyde.

"Ah, so you're feeling better now?"

A soft feminine voice. A Chinese-looking nurse has silently slipped into the room.

"Why am I here? What's happened?"

"There was a gas attack on the underground."

Ah, of course! - all those people collapsing in the train, the strange smell and the revolting taste.

"Have people died? How many? What was the gas? Will I survive?"

"So many questions, Luke! The full casualty figures aren't known yet. *You* should be all right, but you'd better rest, you may be feeling unsteady."

She leans me gently back under the sheets, and I can't help noticing that she too is wearing one of those miracles of micro-engineering under her light blue uniform. Do hospital rules allow that? No doubt Jimmy would say it stimulates the recovery of male patients.

"Now that you're awake, I'll page Dr.Imran".

Oh yes, there was that philosopher's 'intuition' on the radio. Did he know something after all? And what will our government do? Invade another Muslim country, and provoke yet more terrorism? A mustachio'd brown face appears at my bedside.

"Hi Luke! I'm Dr. Imran. How are you feeling?"

"A bit weak, but OK, I think. Was that really a gas attack on the train?"

"Yes, you're lucky to be alive, they used some sort of nerve gas which we're still trying to identify. Those who fell to the floor first had the best chance of surviving: the gas was lighter than air, you see."

"How long have I been in here?"

"You've been unconscious for over 48 hours. We'll have to keep you under observation and do some more tests; we're not sure what's going on in your brain."

He scans the charts at the foot of my bed, humming cheerily to himself.

"So, are you comfortable there?"

"My backside's a bit sore."

"Ah yes, we noticed a bruise from your fall in the train."

"Actually, I tripped in the street as I was running to the station."

"Really? But that does not explain the lipstick all over your face."

He says that with a smile in his voice.

"Oh that ... I seem to remember some female trying to kiss me in the train, and I couldn't escape from her clutches."

"Ho, ho! - a likely story! Well, you've been in the wars one way and another, dear boy. Your bruise will heal, and as you will see, we've removed all trace of the lipstick. But we still need to scan that brain of yours. I suggest you take it very easy for a while. Just call the nurse if you feel unwell."

He vanishes as suddenly as he came. God, I'm one of the lucky ones. Lie back and rest, he said. There's the Cathedral to look at, straight ahead.

**

Suddenly the spire slides smoothly and silently downwards, and disappears from view. A moment later, a huge cloud of grey dust billows up and fills the rectangle of the window. Bits of debris rattle on the glass.

**

Oh my God! Have the jihadists taken to demolishing the symbols of Christianity? I press the panic button at the bedside. Within seconds, the nurse puts her head round the door.

"Did you see that?"

"See what?"

I gesture to the window - but there is the spire, just as before.

"What's going on? Just now, I thought I saw the Cathedral collapse."

"Maybe you're having hallucinations. I'd better call Dr. Imran."

I'm not sure what's real any more. Is this what the gas does? Dr.Imran reappears with miraculous speed.

"Well now, Luke, what's the trouble?"

"I could swear I saw the Cathedral spire slide down in a cloud of dust, just like the Twin Towers on 9/11."

He points to the window, with an expansive gesture.

"As you see, it's still safely there. You must be 'seeing things', as they say in the Highlands. It must be an after-effect of the gas. I'll give you a sedative. Please relax, and don't worry about a thing."

"Dr. Imran, are you from Iraq?"

"How did you guess?"

"Oh, just an intuition."

"Yes, I'm sorry to say I am part of the brain drain from that tortured country. At least here I can save lives, instead of being killed myself. Now, if you'll just drink this little potion for us, it will help you get a good sleep."

It tastes like curried marmalade, with a hint of rotting leaves ... and I'm getting drowsy already.

***

"Ave Maria" is the chant from a procession of robed priests, choristers and incense-bearers, making their way through cobbled streets between overhanging buildings towards the cathedral, followed by a crowd wearing rough cloaks. But suddenly there are shouts and commotion, and stones are thrown. Some of the figures in the procession fall to the ground, while the rest abandon their dignity and hustle each other inside the cathedral. The massive doors are banged shut, and more stones batter on the wood.

***

What a vivid dream! It seemed like something in the Scottish Reformation, when the Protestants did their protesting. We touched on that in History last year. Sectarianism still rears its head at Rangers-Celtic matches; I remember the threatening atmosphere when Jimmy took me to one. Oh, I'm still so sleepy.

***

Who's this kissing my cheek, and dropping tears on my face - it's Mum! Then Dad, who also administers a bristly kiss - that's unusual, from him.

"Luke, darling, we've been so worried about you."

"We've been visiting your unconscious body for the last two days".

"Oh Charles, what a thing to say!"

One of his more inept attempts at humour, I suppose.

"What happened to the other people in the train?"

"The news today said 87 dead, and nearly 200 in hospital."

"God, I'm so lucky."

"The most important thing is that you've survived."

"But what sort of world have I survived into?"

Did that busty female give me the kiss of life? And what happened to her? But I don't feel like filling Mum and Dad in on that bit of the story. But here comes the Chinky nurse again.

"I'm sorry, Dr. Imran recommends that you don't talk to Luke for more than five minutes. His brain needs lots of rest."

"Darling, we'll have to go. We'll be in again every day".

Another kiss from Mum. I'm not used to all this kissing.

***

The sunset is fading, and the floodlights of the Cathedral suddenly switch on, illuminating the spire against the darkening clouds. There it is, still aspiring mutely towards heaven. I wonder what's happening in the outside world. Let's try the radio ... I know that voice - it's that same Islamic philosopher again:

"I am sorry to say that some of my fellow Muslims are misinterpreting the concept of jihad. Yes, it means a struggle between good and evil; but not a war between nations, nor a conflict of civilizations; nor (Allah forbid) a terrorist campaign of indiscriminate slaughter. What jihad should mean for devout Muslims is a constant and balanced effort, a spiritual struggle between the good and evil tendencies in our human nature. The real jihad is within each one of us."

11. THE WIND FROM THE CAIRNGORMS

As soon as they opened the car doors, the wind battered their faces. It was the end of October, they had a free Sunday afternoon, and he had proposed a hill-walk before the winter closes in. She had turned up her nose:

"I don't much feel like it."

"But this might be the last chance of the year."

"There'll be more chances next year, won't there?"

"Yes, but then is then and now is now, and you keep saying how we should live more in the present moment."

"But the weather's cold and grey, and what I would most like in the present moment is to curl up with a good book."

"You can do that all winter. Let's not miss out on the great outdoors, now that we're living in Scotland."

"The great Scottish outdoors can wait a little longer. It'll still be there in May, lighter and warmer."

"Oh, don't be such a wimp."

"Call me a wimp if you must. I just prefer not."

"You always want to have it your own way. Haven't you noticed we're doing fewer and fewer things together?"

"And whose fault is that?"

A tear appeared in her eye.

"Maybe it's both of us. And here's something we *can* do together, this very day. We've nothing else on."

"Oh all right then, let's go for it."

So they drove up one of the Glens of Angus. There wasn't enough daylight left to climb a proper mountain, so he suggested going up to a ridge from where he reckoned there should be a view of the Cairngorms.

"What a wind!" she exclaimed.

"The fresh air is good for you, after those years in London."

"It's a lot fresher than I'd like."

"Let's get moving then, we'll soon warm up."

He led the way up the steep slope. The going was rough from the start, for he'd chosen a route where there was no path. They had to watch every step over the tussocks of heather with boggy bits in between, and half-hidden holes in the ground.

After half an hour's effort they came to a new-looking fence. It was that annoying kind that is too high to step over (unless you're extremely tall!) and so close-wired so that there is no possibility of wriggling under or through. The only way is to climb over, but the strand of barbed wire on top makes that a delicate operation, since you have to force a boot into the lower wiring to get yourself high enough to swing a leg over, while you try to maintain your balance by holding onto the wire, preferably between the barbs. When you get your forward foot over, you have to insert its heel somewhere into the wires on the far side, so that you can swing your other leg over. There is a tendency to wobble at both stages of the operation, and a consequent threat to your private parts. You may opt to attempt the operation where you can hold on to a fencepost, but that has the disadvantage that the barbed wire goes higher there - so most people go for the midpoint between posts. There is a possibility of the irate estate owner or more likely his irate ghillie shouting at you for weakening their expensive fence, and they might order you off their land, as the recently-enacted "right to roam" gives them the right to do if they think you are causing damage. However the chance of that is pretty remote, while the challenge of the barbed wire is unavoidable if you want to proceed

"Do we have to do this?" she said, "haven't we gone far enough?"

"Oh come on. Let's get to the top of the ridge and see the Cairngorms."

"Well, if we must. You'll have to help me, though."

They went for the midpoint option. He got himself over without much difficulty, and then gave her two helping hands, one to hold her leading arm and steady her, the other to still the vibrating barbed wire. But in mid-operation, when she was unstably astride the fence, there came a great gust of wind that took them both by surprise. She lurched towards him, his right hand slipped, a barb punctured his thumb, and his blood spurted onto her jeans.

"This bloody barbed wire," he shouted (and it was quite literally bloody), "C'mon, get your other leg over."

She managed that somehow, and then examined herself. "My new jeans are ruined," she squealed. There was a dark reddish stain, just in the most embarrassing place.

"It'll wash out."

"I don't think so."

"Well, don't let it spoil the day."

"I didn't want to come here in the first place."

"You *are* spoiling it."

"I never thought it would be like this. And look, you're still bleeding. That's a nasty cut, hadn't we better get it washed and bandaged?"

"I'm not giving up now. This will be the first time I've seen the Cairngorms."

He proceeded uphill, sucking his bleeding thumb. She followed slowly and reluctantly, pushing her way through the resistant clumps of heather. They came to a hollow, and she looked down to see how far down her legs the stain had got. But it's always a bad idea when hill-walking to take your eye off your footfall: her right foot squelched into a patch of bright green moss, and the cold brown peaty liquid rose over her ankle and filled her boot.

"Bloody hell!" she shouted; then "Wait!"

He had to retrace his steps.

"My foot is soaked, and it's freezing cold."

"Oh that often happens, the water soon warms up as you walk."

"I've had enough of this godforsaken landscape. I'm not going any further. Give me the keys. I'm going back to the car."

"All right, then. I'll just go to the top and get the view of the Cairngorms."

"You and your wretched Cairngorms. See you in the car."

"Don't insult the Cairngorms. It's not their fault."

"Not very witty. It's your fault for dragging me up here."

She turned on her heel (the left one, which was still dry) and made her way downhill. Meanwhile, relieved of her slowness and foul temper, he bounded up the slope. Pausing for breath half way up the remaining ascent, he looked round and saw that she had got back over the fence - presumably no longer caring what happened to her jeans - and was making a beeline for their car parked at the bottom of the slope.

With a few more minutes of effort he reached the ridge and hopped onto the top of the protuberant rock that had been his aiming point from the start. Where were the Cairngorms, then? The high tops are 4,000 foot plateaux rather than peaks, and the Eastern group are especially elusive from the south: the grey ice-smoothed humps of Ben Avon and Beinn A'Bhuird heave gently into the grey sky and are often hard to distinguish from it, like whalebacks in the sea. But sometimes a shift of the clouds and a gleam of light may pick out the granite tors that decorate the otherwise smooth skin of those remote monsters, like barnacles on whales. He was rewarded with just such a gleam for a few seconds. He said to himself "mission accomplished", and turned to go down into the glen, and home.

But then he felt a sudden chill - for the blue dot of their car had vanished! He looked again. It was definitely not there. Scanning down the road, he thought he glimpsed something disappearing under the trees, but he couldn't be sure. Would she really leave him to find his own way home? She had never done anything like that before. Would she even *be* at home when he eventually got there by hitch-hiking and public transport? He glanced round at the Cairngorms one last time. The gleam had gone, and the sky was darkening. There seemed to be a trace of white around those lofty summits; the first snow of winter. The storm-force wind tore at his hair, and froze his cheeks.

12. SAUCIEHALL STREET

(wi' apologies to Rabbie Burns)

O, ye'll tak' the High Street, and I'll tak' the back lane,
And I'll be in Broonies afore you,
For me and my best fieres will always meet again
In the bonny, bonny bars of MacBroonies.

O, you'll tak' Belhaven, and I'll tak' Macewans,
And I'll get fu' plastered afore you,
And if we feel a need of a wee bit more to drink,
We'll top up wi' a glass of Morangie.

O Jeannie with the light-brown legs,
Ye're teetering on your narrow pins
And look as if ye're going to puke;
May God forgive us all our sins.

You came into the bar so sweet,
An hour ago ye had me randy,
But now my rod's so weak and wet
I couldnae manage houghmagandie.

Tam's oot the door, he's fechtin' fit,
Jus' back fae Afghanistan,
He stumbles bletherin' doon the street,
Followed by the Taliban.

He looks around, he knows they're there,
He hits a drunk, then hits the floor,
The van comes up and loads him in,
The polis's awa' wi' the ex-service man.

13. FROM ATHENS TO THE NORTH

CHARACTERS

"Thrasher" McCuss, an arms salesman

Meinou, Thrasher's wife

Socrates - the Greek philosopher, mysteriously returned to the present day

Callum, a civil servant

Phoebe, a lap dancer
(scene 3 – this part could be played by the same actress as Meinou)

Jason, Thrasher's ten-year-old son

Mr.Jones, nightclub manager + immigration official
    (small parts in scenes 3 & 5)

Nightclub bouncer + policeman
(small parts in scenes 3 & 5)

There is a visual part throughout for a computer screen

SCENE 1

"Thrasher" McCuss sits writing at his desk, with his back to the audience, in a crowded untidy office in the South Gyle Industrial Estate at the edge of Edinburgh. **'Ping'** *goes his computer. There is a screen on the wall behind him (big enough for the audience to read what appears on it) and the message comes up:*

New e-mail for Mr. T. McCuss

Without looking up, Thrasher hits a key, and the screen now shows:

How many JB21's next month? We need to re-order today. Derek

After some more scribbling, Thrasher looks at the screen, then rapidly types in:

They're going fast - better say 10,000. Thrasher

As he is does this, the phone rings:

THRASHER. Hello ... yes, speaking ... "Thrasher"? - Oh, that's just a nickname, my mates thought I was so fast on the computer and on sales. What can I do for you? ... Yes, I know Mr. Mushadoo, he's been one of our best customers, any friend of his is a friend of ours ... What, that many? I'll have to ask my colleague how soon we can do that ... export licence? Not a problem, in my experience ... yes, I know there are those regulations, but we find they're hardly ever enforced ... *(laughs)* Yes, we're all contributing to the economy, aren't we? A pleasure to speak to you, Mr. ...? Mr.Guntrip. ... Hey – that's a great name! I'll get back to you soon about your guns.

During this conversation, the computer pings again:

New e-mail for Mr. T. McCuss

Thrasher hits a key whilst talking, and the message is:

Please meet Socrates at Turnhouse today 16.20 on flight BCE399

When the phone call is finished, Thrasher looks at the message and scratches his head.

THRASHER. That's odd. Who the heck is this from?

He scrolls up the screen and finds:

sender: AOTTA.com@athens.gr

THRASHER. Never heard of them. 'AOTTA' sounds Greek. Let's google them:

What comes up is:

AOTTA - the Almost Omniscient Time Travel Agency. First registered: Athens 470 BCE

THRASHER. That's an original cover-story. Better check them out.

He types in:

Reply from: T.McCuss@northernsecurities.com
Re: 50 crates arriving Edinburgh today. Please quote order number.

Then he picks up the phone:

THRASHER. Hello, Derek, I've had a Mr.Guntrip on the phone. He wants a thousand AK47's as soon as poss. What can we do for him? ... Yes, it'll take a while, obviously, they're in demand all over the place ... OK, I'll tell him, half payment up front. Oh, and while you're there, Derek, I've just had a peculiar e-mail about a delivery from Greece arriving at the airport this afternoon. Do you know anything about people called AOTTA? ... no, nor have I ... yeah, yeah, I'm checking, of course.

Thrasher stretches, gets up and paces round the room, and makes himself a cup of coffee. While he does so, his computer pings yet again:

New e-mail for Mr. T. McCuss

He opens the message:

Re: Socrates arriving Turnhouse 16.20
Our research department has established that your wife Meinou is the nearest living descendant of our client Socrates. He has expressed a wish to meet his family. We are sure you will understand.

THRASHER. Good grief! This is getting weirder and weirder ... And it says *So*crates is arriving. *[he pronounces it to rhyme with 'slow crates']* I thought they said '50 crates' first time.

He picks up the phone again:

THRASHER. Derek, I've just got an even stranger reply from these AOTTA people. No order number, just an implausible story about some fellow wanting to meet my wife. ... A threat? My God, could they be planning to take her hostage?   But how would they know about *her*? ... Yes, we first met at The Philosopher's Bar in Athens ten years ago ... (*angrily*) No, I have no doubts about her past ... I know we've done some good business through the Greeks,

103

but this one smells funny to me. ... OK, if you say so, Derek, I'll go out to the airport and see what it's all about.

Thrasher paces up and down, then suddenly takes out his mobile and uses it.

THRASHER. Hi, darling, what are you up to?

Meinou's picture comes upon the screen (Thrasher is using a phone/picture facility on his computer). She is jogging down a street in suburban Edinburgh, in a fetching Lycra outfit.

MEINOU. *(breathily)* Oh, hi there. How nice to have your attention in the daytime - but you'll have to be quick, I'm on my way to my yoga class.

THRASHER. OK, OK, just tell me, have you ever heard of someone called 'So-crates'? *[he still pronounces it like 'slow crates']* He claims to be a relative of yours.

MEINOU. That name doesn't mean anything to me. Spell it.

THRASHER. S-O-C-R-A-T-E-S.

MEINOU. Oh, *Socrates*, you ignoramus! He was a philosopher in ancient Athens, four centuries before Christ. But I don't have any relatives with that name – it isn't used in Greece now. What's this all this about, anyway?

THRASHER. I got this strange e-mail asking me to meet someone called Socrates at the airport.

MEINOU. Well, you'd better go and talk to this so-called philosopher then - maybe you'll learn something! But if he turns out to be one of your shifty dealers, please don't bring him home, we need a break from all that. Must run now or I'll be late for my first posture. Byee.

SCENE 2

Thrasher is back in his office, together with Socrates, a grey-haired but vigorous man with a huge nose and prominent eyes, dressed in a white robe (a toga). He speaks English with a strange but perfectly intelligible accent.

THRASHER. Well, Mr. Socrates, welcome to my humble office. You must be tired after your flight – it's four hours from Athens, isn't it? Can I give you a cup of coffee?

SOCRATES. Coffee? What is that?

THRASHER. Is it not allowed in your country? I recommend it. I couldn't work without it, it aids my concentration.

SOCRATES. I will try; I am interested in new experiences - especially if they involve concentration. Thank you. *[He takes a gulp, and smiles broadly]* Yes, it is strong stuff indeed, but not as good as our Greek wines.

THRASHER. Oh, you mean Rezina - I've tried that in Greece with Meinou. She laps the stuff up, but I never acquired the taste. I prefer my alcohol without tree-juice.

SOCRATES. So you have been to my country? I have been reliably informed that your wife Meinou is my nearest living relative. If so, you and I are family.

THRASHER. *(guardedly)* That surprises me - I can neither confirm nor deny that suggestion. I'll have to ask Meinou about it. ... But since you're here on business, what can we do for you? Would you like to see some of our displays?

SOCRATES. Certainly, I would like to know what you do, and why you do it. I'm always willing to learn.

THRASHER. Well, we do small arms and rocket launchers, and we have good contacts for landmines.

SOCRATES. I am not sure I understand all those words. Please explain to me what these landmines do.

THRASHER. You're not sure what a landmine is? Have you come to the right address? But perhaps you're unsure of your English? We sometimes have to assist our clients to communicate. *(Socrates nods gravely.)* All right then, I'll show you some of our publicity material on screen:

Landmines contain high explosive, set off by a pressure-sensitive trigger. A line of landmines provides an effective screen against penetration by infantry or vehicles.

Now if that's what you want, we can help. I know there's an international ban on them, but we have ways of getting around that. The cheapest is the JT509, then there's the AQ462, and the tank-busting TB111.

SOCRATES. I can see you are a keen salesman, but am I to understand that a landmine will kill whoever treads on it?

THRASHER. Well, it may not always kill outright, but it certainly puts a soldier out of action.

SOCRATES. That seems rather unsporting. In our army, the only honorable way to kill was with swords or javelins. It was a man-on-man thing, and every soldier had the chance to defend himself.

THRASHER. But as you know, in modern warfare the rules have changed. You will find our products extremely effective.

SOCRATES. I fear so. These landmines, as you call them, will explode in response to any pressure?

THRASHER. Yes, anything heavier than a rat.

SOCRATES. So if they are hidden in the ground, they will kill or injure anyone who treads on them - even children?

THRASHER. I'm afraid so. The media sometimes show sad pictures of children who've lost limbs, but that's not *my* business.

SOCRATES. But it is how you earn your living.

THRASHER. I can't be responsible for how our products are used. It's a competitive market, and we have to work our socks off to stay in business.

SOCRATES. So you think it is right to sell these devices?

THRASHER. I know they're supposed to be illegal, but that hasn't been contested in the courts - and there's still plenty of demand for them.

SOCRATES. That is not what I meant. Do you think it is *right*?

THRASHER. It's in the interests of our company - and it's how I support my family.

SOCRATES. So whatever is in your self-interest is right?

THRASHER. It's every man for himself in this world.

SOCRATES. Are you so sure you *know* what's in your own self-interest?

THRASHER. Surely I'm the best judge of that?

SOCRATES. Do you consider yourself as one individual, distinct from all others?

THRASHER. Look, Mr.Socrates, we don't do philosophy here. ... But that reminds me of a TV programme about selfish genes I saw the other night. I guess I judge by the advantage primarily to myself, but also to the people I'm related to, in proportion to the genes I share with them.

SOCRATES. What are genes?

THRASHER. Oh, you know, everyone talks about them these days. I'm not sure of the exact definition, but it's something to do with what we inherit at birth from our parents.

SOCRATES. Where does that leave Meinou? I take it you don't share genes with her.

THRASHER. Well, I'm still fond of her, despite our occasional tiffs. And she's the mother of my son, so we mix our genes together, if you see what I mean. ... Now Mr. Socrates, it's a pleasure to talk philosophy with you, but shall we get down to business?

SOCRATES. But this *is* the business *I* do. If you apply your business philosophy to the rest of your life, how does that work out? For example, when you promised to stay with your wife until death, is your commitment conditional on her good behaviour - where 'good' means what is to your advantage?

THRASHER. That's a rather crude way of putting it. Things are usually OK between us. But I suppose when a relationship breaks down, it's rational to get out of it.

SOCRATES. And what about your children? Does your commitment to *them* also depend on their behaving to your advantage?

THRASHER. We've only got the one child, so far. And his behaviour is sometimes pretty awful: there are times when I could gladly do without him.

SOCRATES. Suppose you never saw him again?

THRASHER. *(shifting in his chair)* I suppose I'd miss him. ... Hang on, is that supposed to be a threat? *(stands up)*

SOCRATES. Not in the least, my dear fellow. All I do is ask questions. I just want to understand. *(Thrasher sits down again.)*

THRASHER. Look, Mr. Socrates, I thought you came here to do business with us. If you're not interested in buying, then I've got other things to do.

SOCRATES. My business is to understand, and help others understand.

The phone rings:

THRASHER. Oh, hello, Callum ... God, is that the time? I've been talking to a client here ... OK, see you there.

He stares at his strange visitor, wondering what to do with him.

THRASHER. Mr. Socrates, I have to go and meet someone in town. Have you got another appointment in Edinburgh?

SOCRATES. If you remember, my hope was to meet your wife.

THRASHER. Oh really? I'd forgotten about that story. But to be honest, she's not keen on socializing with my clients. What are your plans? Have you got somewhere to stay?

SOCRATES. I do not make plans. This city is foreign to me, and I was hoping that my family might extend hospitality to a long-lost relative. *(He smiles broadly, and his eyes flash)*

THRASHER. Well, I can't leave you here. I suppose you'd better come with me, and we'll see what we can sort out for you.

SCENE 3

In a club in the Stockbridge area of Edinburgh. There is an alcove, with easy chairs around it. On the wall there is an illuminated screen that reads:

**Welcome to The Northern Light Club.
Let us throw new light on what you most desire**

(on the background of the screen, pole dancers are writhing)

Thrasher and Socrates are shown to a table, where Callum is already sitting.

THRASHER. *(to Socrates)* This is my friend Callum. He's in the Department of Trade and Industry, Export Services Division - but despite that he's quite good company. *(to Callum)* This is Mr. Socrates, a very special customer from Athens.

CALLUM. Socrates, eh? I remember that name from when I studied philosophy at St.Andrews. Wasn't he the one who went around annoying people by asking philosophical questions, and they had to make him drink the hemlock to stop his questioning? I didn't know the name was still used in Greece. Anyway, Mr. Socrates, welcome to "the Athens of the North"! Did you know that Edinburgh earned that title when it was the centre of the Scottish Enlightenment in the 18th century?

SOCRATES. *(smiles benignly)* No, I did not know that. It is always a pleasure to learn.

THRASHER. Would you believe it, Callum? Mr. Socrates and I have been having an ethical discussion!

CALLUM. *(roars with laughter)* You, Thrasher, of all people, taking lessons in ethics? That's rich!

THRASHER. Well, he did made me think.

CALLUM. *(looks at Thrasher with surprise)* Don't think *too* hard, it's not good for business. (*a waitress comes to take their order)* Mr. Socrates, what can I get you to drink?

SOCRATES. Local piety would suggest the local wine.

CALLUM. Actually, they don't make wine in Edinburgh – not yet, anyway, despite what the climate change fanatics tell us. The traditional Scottish drink is whisky. May I suggest that local piety would indicate a Highland Malt? Which would you recommend, Thrasher?

THRASHER. Oh, you're the expert, Callum. You choose.

CALLUM. OK then. Shall we all have one? The Glen Morangie, please. Double measures, darling.

THRASHER. Have a crisp, Mr. Socrates, while we're waiting?

Socrates takes a huge handful of crisps, stuffs them into his mouth with one movement, and crunches them noisily. Fragments fall down his toga, and he brushes them off. His eyes twinkle. Then the drinks come.

CALLUM. (*lifts his glass*) To the Athens-Edinburgh connection!

SOCRATES. To the gods of hospitality, across space and time!

Socrates takes a large swig of whisky, downs it, and just manages to control a splutter, but without any other effect except a greater intensity in his impressive eyes. Callum and Thrasher exchange smiles, and sip theirs more slowly.

SOCRATES. This is stronger than that coffee!

THRASHER. Yes, you can't beat Scottish whisky. "The water of life", as they say. Would you like another?

Socrates declines gracefully. Then a girl in a sequinned outfit sidles up to their table and simpers:

PHOEBE. Good evening, gentlemen. My name is Phoebe. I hope you are enjoying your drinks?

CALLUM. Very much, thank you, Phoebe - and what can you offer us tonight?

PHOEBE. Well, I do a belly-dance for a tenner, a topless treat for £20, or the full Phoebe for £30 - plus whatever gratuities you may care to add.

SOCRATES. What is she talking about?

THRASHER. She will dance for us … erotically.

SOCRATES. In my time it was usually young boys who did that … well, I am learning.

CALLUM. Mr. Socrates, since you have travelled so far for our mutual benefit, allow me to treat you to the full Phoebe.

He produces three notes, Phoebe pushes forward a shapely thigh, and he slips them into her strategically-placed garter. Rhythmic music emanates from the walls, and the screen display changes:

Your desire is our pleasure
ENJOY
but for reasons of hygiene and decorum
please remember our rule
NO TOUCHING

Phoebe begins her routine. The centre of her outfit splits, revealing an orange- tanned abdomen which starts to writhe lasciviously in front of Socrates. He smiles broadly. Then she begins to peel off her costume. Underneath there is just some black stringy stuff. Bluish lighting effects ripple over her skin. Trying to follow the beat of the music, she toys with the upper section of her apparatus, and soon a nipple is wobbling a few inches from Socrates' face. His smile fades somewhat. She cavorts around the table offering a similar display to each customer, then she plants herself between Socrates' legs and begins untwisting the remaining wisps of material as she gyrates. His smile disappears, and his eyes flash:

SOCRATES. Phoebe, why are you doing this?

She stops for a moment, then tries to continue:

PHOEBE. Aren't you enjoying it, sir?

SOCRATES. Well, I suppose it arouses appetite, even in a man of my age - though I must say I find it *more* erotic when something is left to the imagination. But I presume you are not really doing it for *me*. It's like serving what your menu calls an appetizer, but without the main course - which is not so pleasing after all!

PHOEBE. What? Oh, I see what you mean. Well, of course - what did you expect? The rule of the house is: no touching.

SOCRATES. So there's nothing personal about this. You don't get to know people here, do you?

Phoebe was still trying to go through her motions as this conversation proceeded, but by now she is quite put off her rhythm.

PHOEBE. Actually, we're not supposed to talk to customers, after the initial chat.

SOCRATES. So you bare your body, but not your soul?

PHOEBE. I wouldn't want to bare my soul to the people who come in here. I only do this for the money.

SOCRATES. Just as I thought. And why do you need the money?

PHOEBE. I'm at an English university, and I've got to pay tuition fees.

SOCRATES. And what are you studying?

PHOEBE. Philosophy. *(she admits, with an embarrassed smile)*

SOCRATES. Ah, *philo-sophia*: the love of wisdom.

At this moment, the music and lightshow are switched off, and the screen display abruptly changes to:

> **You have broken the house rules**
> **Please leave immediately**
> **Our staff will be pleased to assist you**
> **No refunds will be given**

Two men in dinner suits approach the table. One of them is of formidable size.

BOUNCER. What's going on here?

THRASHER. It's all right, he was only having a philosophical dialogue with her.

BOUNCER. Oh yeah, that's what they all say.

MR. JONES. Hi, Callum, nice to see you again - but you must explain the rules to your guests.

PHOEBE. He didn't touch me, Mr. Jones, he only *talked*.

JONES. Why have you stopped dancing, then?

PHOEBE. He touched my mind.

JONES. You'd better forget about your mind here, and concentrate on your body.

PHOEBE. Actually, I'm not sure I want to do this any more.

JONES. Oh really? Well, that's your privilege, darling. There's plenty more out there to take your place. *(to his bouncer)* This fellow's corrupting my young dancers. See him out, will you?

An ugly smile indicates delight in the bouncer's ejaculatory role. He hoists Socrates to his feet and propels him rapidly out of the room. As they approach the door, Socrates shouts:

SOCRATES. Phoebe, I wish you *sophia*.

At the door, a large foot is applied to Socrates' backside, and when his face hits the cobbles outside he shouts with pain. Thrasher catches up with him and tries to stop the bleeding from his nose.

THRASHER. C'mon, I'd better take you home.

Callum stands watching in the doorway, talking on his mobile phone.

SCENE 4

In the McCuss's modest house in Craigleith Crescent, Edinburgh EH4. Downstairs, Socrates lies asleep on the sofa, wrapped up in his toga. Upstairs, Thrasher is waking up beside Meinou, wondering how to break the news to her there is a visiting Greek of mysterious purpose sleeping in the living room. He yawns, stretches, and kisses Meinou on the forehead. She moans, and turns over. After a while, he kisses the back of her neck

THRASHER. Meinou ... Meinou.

She groans, turns over again, and opens one eye.

THRASHER. *(tentatively)* Don't take this amiss, my sweet, but there's someone downstairs who claims to be your long-lost relative.

MEINOU. *(sits up in bed suddenly, and shouts)* What? Pull the other one! Don't tell me you've brought home another of your tedious clients!

THRASHER. But this one's different. He's called 'Socrates' - remember, we talked about him on the phone. We haven't actually done any business yet, but I can't help liking him, he has such a charming way of asking difficult questions.

MEINOU. We have enough difficult questions in this house already. And I *told* you to give us a break from your people.

THRASHER. But he claims to be one of *your* people! We took him to a club last night, and he got thrown out, and he had nowhere else to go.

MEINOU. Worse and worse! I dread to think what sort of club you and your shady clients go to. And then you bring back this drunken riotous foreigner and let him into our house?

THRASHER. He wasn't drunken or riotous in the least. All he did was ask unusual questions. And he claims to be related to you … and come to think of it, maybe there is something Greek about him.

MEINOU. Greek or not, I think you've been taken for a ride. There are plenty of Greeks I wouldn't let inside my house.

THRASHER. Well, he's here, anyway. You'd better meet him, and see what you think.

Meinou throws on a dressing gown, and goes downstairs in a foul mood. Thrasher does the same.

THRASHER. Mr. Socrates, this is my wife, who you were so keen to meet.

Socrates starts, and struggles to his feet; he pulls his bloodstained toga around himself, and looks Meinou slowly and carefully in the face. Then he kisses her hand in a formal way, and says in his curious accent:

SOCRATES. Meinou, I can see the light of Greece in your eyes. I have been informed that you are my nearest living descendant. I am come to inquire if virtue is still being taught in your generation.

MEINOU. I know of no relative by your name. Which generation would you be, then?

SOCRATES. Over a hundred generations ago.

MEINOU. You cannot be serious! Is this some kind of con-trick? And I've no idea what you mean by that stuff about virtue. … But you're bleeding - here, let me clean up your face. *(She wets a paper towel and dabs his face)* Did you get into a fight last night?

THRASHER. No, he got himself thrown out of the club - just for talking.

MEINOU. *(as she dries Socrates' face)* That must have been quite some talking. What did you say?

SOCRATES. I ask people what they are doing, and why they are doing it.

MEINOU. Really? I can well imagine that could get you into all sorts of trouble.

SOCRATES. So I have found. Yet it seems the most important thing I can do.

Suddenly Thrasher and Meinou's ten-year-old son Jason bounces in, and shouts:

JASON. Dad, can you take me to the football this afternoon?

THRASHER. *(groans)* We haven't decided yet.

SOCRATES. So this is the hundred-and-first generation?

THRASHER. This is Jason.

SOCRATES. Delighted to meet you, Jason. *(offering a handshake, which Jason shyly accepts)* If your parents permit, I would like to talk with you too. I would like to know what you are learning.

JASON. *(to his parents' surprise)* OK.

MEINOU. *(applying a bandage to Socrates' nose)* Well, maybe later. But first we all need some breakfast.

They sit round the table. Socrates is intrigued by the range of foods on offer, and takes a liberal helping of Coco-pops.

SOCRATES. What are these? Are they like those crisps you gave me last night, Mr. Thrasher?

MEINOU. "Mr. Thrasher"! I like that – he is a bit of a thrasher!

THRASHER. Actually, they're a bit more substantial, and they're sweet - but I doubt if they're any more nutritious.

Socrates wolfs them down.

JASON. Don't they have Coco-pops where you live? Where *do* you live, Mr. Socrates?

SOCRATES. In Athens.

JASON. Where's that?

SOCRATES. In Greece.

JASON. Where's that?

SOCRATES. You don't know where Greece is? I am surprised.

MEINOU. So am I.

SOCRATES. It is a long way south of here, on the Mediterranean Sea, where it's much warmer.

JASON. But no Cocopops?

SOCRATES. No - not in my time, anyway.

THRASHER. Would you like tea or coffee, Mr. Socrates?

SOCRATES. Well, I had coffee yesterday, so perhaps I will try the tea. But I hope it's not as strong as the whisky, I don't feel ready for any more of that this morning.

JASON. You've never had tea before? You're weird.

MEINOU. Jason, be polite to our guest – whether invited or not *(with a glare at Thrasher).*

SOCRATES. I see the woman still rules in the household! Xanthippe was the just the same, she wouldn't allow any philosophical discussion at home.

MEINOU. Quite right, too. Now, Thrasher, we've got to get dressed, there's the shopping to do, and I've got an appointment with the hairdresser - and you'll be taking Jason to the football later, won't you?

THRASHER. *(sighs)* Yes, I suppose so. Now Mr. Socrates, as you see, we are quite busy on a Saturday.

MEINOU. *(to Socrates)* Perhaps we can give you a lift, and drop you off where you want to go?

SOCRATES. At this moment, there is nowhere that I want to go. I like to feel at home wherever I am.

MEINOU. Well, Mr. Socrates, I don't want to appear inhospitable to travellers, but we have a lot to do today. Maybe you can talk to Jason here, while we get dressed?

SOCRATES. Nothing would give me greater pleasure - not that my own pleasure is the most important thing, of course.

Thrasher and Meinou disappear upstairs.

SCENE 5

SOCRATES. *(after a thoughtful interval)* Well, Jason, do you know that you and I are related?

JASON. I've never heard of you before.

SOCRATES. If you think about it, we all have lots of relatives we have never heard of before – I mean, all those great-great-grandparents, and so on.

JASON. I suppose so. But they're all *dead*.

SOCRATES. Yes, indeed - or so we think. But there must also be lots of *living* relatives we don't know – third and fourth cousins, et cetera.

JASON. Yes, but they're not real relatives, are they?

SOCRATES. Just because you don't know them, that doesn't mean they're not related to you.

JASON. I guess so.

SOCRATES. So if you go far enough back, maybe everyone is related to everyone else?

JASON. I never thought of it that way.

SOCRATES. So probably I am related to you after all?

JASON. OK, OK - whatever. Does it matter?

SOCRATES. Well, maybe not that much - but what *is* important is that you and I are talking now. Tell me, Jason, what would you be doing if I wasn't here?

JASON. Uh, probably playing on my computer.

SOCRATES. 'Computer' – what is *that*?

JASON. I can't believe you don't know what a computer is! Don't they have them in your country?

SOCRATES. I am discovering that you have many things we did not have. But do you have what's most important, I wonder?

JASON. What's more important than a computer?

SOCRATES. We'll see. Can you show me one?

Jason takes Socrates over to a desk by the wall, and switches on the computer. The screen (visible to the audience) comes up with:

Jason McCuss:
his programmes

SOCRATES. More words on shiny surfaces. So what can you do with this?

JASON. All sorts of things. Would you like to play a game?

SOCRATES. Oh, yes. I love games.

JASON. Well, here's one I like. *(He hits the keys and brings up a game)* You have to try to keep the car on the road, no matter how fast it goes, and you win a prize if you get to the end without crashing. *(he demonstrates)*

SOCRATES. Amazing! How do they produce all those shapes and colours and make them move so fast?

JASON. I dunno. But it's fun, isn't it? Would you like a shot?

SOCRATES. All right then. What am I supposed to do?

JASON. You have to touch this key to make it turn left, this one to go right, this one to make it go up, and this one to keep it down. Ready? I'll start it for you. *(loud music)*

SOCRATES. Here I go ... but why all that noise? ... Whoops ... Oh   Eeeeeh – I've crashed already! Can I have another try? ... Aah ... Woe ... Oh Zeus - I'm crashed again
!
JASON. Zeus - who's Zeus?

SOCRATES. You haven't heard of Zeus? What do they teach the young these days? In our Greek popular religion, Zeus is the chief of the gods.

JASON. I never heard of religion being popular. You're weird.

SOCRATES. I think I will take that as a compliment. May I have one more try at this game? I was just beginning to learn how to do it ... *(this time he manages to get to the end, and laughs uproariously).*

JASON. You see, that grade is easy. Shall we try a faster speed?

SOCRATES. No thank you, Jason, that is quite fast enough for my aging brain.

Meinou comes downstairs again, dressed rather elegantly. Thrasher follows, in jeans. Jason goes back to his computer.

MEINOU. Well, Mr. Socrates, what do you make of the hundred-and-first generation?

SOCRATES. He showed me what he does on that screen, and we played one of his games. It was fun, though I found the music very noisy (what does it do the soul, I wonder?) He has some innate talent, it just needs bringing out. But it seems what he most wants to do is look at those screens.

MEINOU. He'll spend all his time that way, if we let him.

SOCRATES. Watching mere shadows – it's like living in a cave, not knowing anything about the reality outside.

MEINOU. That's a good way of putting it. And what annoys me most is the advertisements they include with the children's programmes, so that kids want to go out and get all that stuff.

SOCRATES. Who decides what images are put before the young? Whoever they are, they have great power. How can virtue ever be taught?

MEINOU. Yes, it worries me too. One feels so helpless.

SOCRATES. Surely not? It's harder than teaching mathematics, I know, but we have to believe that everyone has a potential for good and that we can do something to bring it out.

MEINOU. *(with tears forming in her eyes)* Mr. Socrates, I'm almost beginning to believe ...

But at that moment there is a loud knock at the front door. Thrasher answers it. A man in a suit stands there, accompanied by a uniformed policeman. The suit holds up a plastic card:

OFFICIAL. Home Office Immigration Department. Is there a Mr. Crates here?

THRASHER. 'Crates?' ... Oh, I suppose you mean Socrates.

OFFICIAL. That'll be him. We need to see him, *now*.

(Thrasher shows them in, and indicates Socrates) Are you Mr. S. O. Crates, of Athens, Greece?

SOCRATES. If you pronounce that as one word - 'Socrates' - yes, I am he.

OFFICIAL. The Home Secretary has determined that your presence in the United Kingdom is not conducive to the national interest. I must therefore require you to accompany me to the airport for deportation. You have ten minutes to pack your bags.

SOCRATES. I have no bags. I am ready now.

POLICEMAN. Come along then, Mr.Crates. We haven't got all day.

They accompany him out of the front door.
Thrasher and Meinou sit down at the table, feeling drained.

MEINOU. Oh my God, it almost began to feel as if he was the real Socrates.

THRASHER. But that's absurd - how could anyone reappear two thousand years after their death?

MEINOU. Well, whoever he was, he was awfully like what I've heard about the Socrates of ancient Athens. He kept making me think - and I couldn't help feeling he was right.

THRASHER. Yes, I know how you feel . . . *(long pause)* ...
I wonder if I can get out of this business.

MEINOU. It seems we *are* out of it. He's been deported.

THRASHER. No I don't mean that. I mean *my* business.

MEINOU. What? Give up your job? But what would we do for money? We've got a mortgage to pay.

THRASHER. I'd have to find something else ... it might take some time.

JASON *(re-entering).* Who was that Mr. Socrates? He was interesting.

THRASHER. Yes, I rather liked him too, despite his difficult questions. He's gone, and it looks like he won't be coming back. ... But we can e-mail his company, I remember their address.

He sits down and types at the keyboard; and after a few seconds the message comes up:

sender: AOTTA. com @athens.gr
re: Socrates

This company ceased trading in 399 BCE, and no more messages will be answered. Any further enquiries should be directed to Plato.

14. GOOD HEAVENS!

Surely that wasn't my alarm clock? It was more like the blast of a trumpet, loud enough to waken the dead:

Tatata-taa ... tatata-too ... tatata-tee.

Then the memory came back: a sharp pain in my chest, and I was flat on my back on the kitchen floor. Debussy ambled over with her tail up and sniffed at my face, but I couldn't lift a finger to her.

But where was I now? I seemed to be moving effortlessly through empty space. My skin had turned into smooth grey plastic, and my private parts had gone. My belly was flattened, but that didn't seem like sufficient compensation. Then I glimpsed a crowd of similarly grey humanoids whizzing along in front of me, each with a set of transparent wings attached to their shoulder-blades, like dragon-flies. That explained the faint whine I heard - I had wings too. I joined the swarm, but where we were going, God only knew. I glanced at my fellow-fliers. Their eyes were enlarged, but their faces had human individuality and expressiveness, and most of them retained their hair. Their bodies all looked much the same at first, but on discreet inspection I could distinguish some as female by slightly wider hips and vestigial bulges on the chest.

Amongst the swarm, I thought I glimpsed a familiar face. Wasn't that Kevin, my enthusiastic Anglican friend with whom I'd enjoyed so many theological arguments? He had no trouble identifying *me*, for he flew over with a broad smile on his little grey face:

"Lionel! It's great to see you up here. I told you so! It is God's will that all who respond to Him should be saved - even sceptics."

"Kevin! You mean to say we're in heaven? Trust you to turn up, then! But is this really salvation, this flitting around through empty space?"

"Wait and see. This is surely only the beginning."

"But what are we supposed to do with these funny little sexless bodies?"

"They must be the *spiritual* bodies that St. Paul wrote about in 1 *Corinthians* 15. We are not disembodied souls, we are resurrected bodies. We carry memories of our life on earth, and everyone is recognizably the same person as they were."

I wasn't so sure that I felt the same person as before, what with the heart attack and the castration. I asked Kevin:

"What happened to *you*? How come we arrived here at the same time?"

"Oh, I fell under the proverbial bus - quite literally. I was crossing the High Street in the middle of theological debate with one of those over-keen graduate students, and I failed to see a minibus of Chinese tourists. But I don't mind, I had a good life. Mary is well provided for, and she can have a well-earned rest from me until she joins us up here. And we have all eternity to look forward to."

I felt less enthusiastic about the prospect. I wasn't happy about the way my body had been spiritualized. Not that sex had been the most important thing in my life - that was music - but it was the obvious candidate for *second* most important thing.

As we whizzed along, the air thickened with yet more human dragonflies, and soon we were in the midst of an aerial traffic jam. Ahead I could glimpse a pearly white surface, like the side of a cruise liner.

"Why is heaven so crowded?" I asked.

"Well, the population of the earth has increased, and God wants as many as possible to be saved."

A flashing sign now appeared:

Now admitting DNA nos. from

and the number blinking in the box was:

2804756396841

"Ah", said Kevin, "I see they've modernized the entry procedure - just as you would expect from omniscience!"

"How are we supposed to know our DNA codes?"

"I'm sure they've thought of that."

We joined a jostling crowd around a small circular portal in that pearly wall. People were flying *backwards* towards it, the door opened to admit them, then shut again quickly.

"Oh, I get it", exclaimed Kevin. "Our numbers must be stamped on our backs. Can you see mine?"

There was indeed a bar-code, just under his wings. Some wit had scrawled in 'Best before 2010'.

When Kevin's turn came, he got in on the first attempt. Typical, I thought, promotion always came easily to him. But when my turn came, nothing happened though I presented my posterior from various angles (new technology never did seem to work for me). The buzz from the swarm grew impatient. I began to panic. Was I not qualified for heaven after all? Would I be sent to a far less salubrious place? Little grey hands pointed me towards the small print:

In case of difficulty
apply to St. Peter
at the Porter's Lodge

I followed the arrow and came to a large wooden gate, like that of an Oxford college. Set within the gate was a door, and beside it was a high handle (old technology, indeed). I pulled the handle, and a bell tinkled. Nothing happened. My anxiety rose again. I yanked once more. Presently there came a sound of shuffling feet, a cracked voice said:

"Patience is a virtue"

The door creaked open to reveal an extremely old man with a huge bald head. He was dressed in flowing robes with a bunch of keys round his waist.

"Yes?"

"I'm having trouble getting in", I said, urgently.

"Oh, they all say that", he replied.

"Yes, but I thought I was qualified."

"What is your problem, then?"

"I just couldn't get the portal to open for me."

"Ah, this new-fangled technology! We had to introduce it because the numbers were getting so high. But I still have to deal with problem cases myself. There's no escaping the human factor, even here."

"Well, can you do anything for me?" I asked.

"So you think you're admitted, do you? I'll have to check with the Management about your case. You'd better flit over here and perch with your back to me so I can read them your number."

There followed a lengthy interchange in a mysterious heavenly language like nothing I had heard before. My eternal fate remained on tenterhooks. But eventually St. Peter's face broke into a smile:

"Yes, sir, your number *is* on the list. Welcome to heaven!"

I was lost for words; this was something for which I had no precedent. The good saint suddenly became more affable:

"You see, sir, we have to discriminate. I know that's become a politically incorrect word down below, but we have to draw the line somewhere, even if there's not much difference at the borderline. I wouldn't know the details of your case, sir, but once you're admitted we treat you all the same. ... Now sir, if you'll just fly up towards that circle there."

I flitted obediently, and the hole opened. I perched on the window-ledge, and looked around a college quad glowing with unearthly light.

"If you fly over there, above the Chapel", said the aged Saint, "you'll catch up with the other entrants. But there's no need to hurry, you have all eternity before you. Enjoy!"

St. Peter's change of tone gave me confidence. A feeling of pride flooded over me on my admission to this august institution about which I'd heard so much - though I had a sneaking suspicion that I might be one of those who only *just* qualified. I caught up with my swarm just as they flew towards another sign:

Induction for new entrants

We flitted in through an open door and found ourselves in an enormous lecture-theatre, with perching-poles instead of benches. When a vigorous figure flew in with a black gown billowing behind him, all noise ceased. Hanging from his neck was an identification badge, and below his photograph I could make out the words:

St. Paul
Heavenly Professor
of Evangelical Theology

"My name is Paul", he said, in ringing tones that easily reached the back row, "and it is my pleasant duty to welcome you into heaven. You are justified in the sight of God, and spiritual fulfillment awaits you. But it remains for you to discover what that means."

He paused to fold his wings, which had still been vibrating.

"First, however, there are some housekeeping matters you should know about. You will be glad to hear that we run an energy-efficient economy here. Your input will almost balance your output. Your new spiritual bodies need next to nothing, but those wings do use a little energy. You will find that all that you require is the occasional sip of ambrosia, and dispensers are located at convenient intervals. If you are such a frequent flier as to run low in between dispensers, I'm sure you will find a good Samaritan to give you a lift."

"So we never get to *eat*?" I whispered to Kevin.

"Apparently not", he said.

"So there'll be no need to excrete?"

"I heard that", thundered St. Paul. "It seems there are some misconceptions that need correction. You are now living in the Spirit, not in the Flesh. You have bodies, yes, but they are *spiritualized*. You have left behind the flesh, with its needs, desires and lusts."

"The next thing you need to know", continued our Heavenly Professor, "is about the angels. They are disembodied spirits, and they enjoy close relations with the Divine Trinity - at least, the ones up here do", he added darkly. "Each of you is assigned a guardian angel who will monitor your spiritual progress. You may wonder how angels get in touch with you. Well, it may not happen very often, but you will hear a high-pitched voice inside your head which you will find it difficult to ignore. If you wish to seek spiritual counsel, we have provided a heavenly telephone service. You will find phone booths where, if you present your barcode, you will be connected to your angelic adviser. Heavenly Management considered at their last Board Meeting whether to introduce mobile phones, but we decided that we don't want you going round holding little boxes to your heads half the time; we prefer that you be fully and spiritually present in whatever place you are at."

Someone in the second row raised a grey arm.

"Forgive me, sir, but it seems that you haven't answered the question of how to get in touch with an angel. For if a spirit is truly disembodied, he or she (or it?) has no *ear* to put to the phone, and not even a *brain* to be affected by physical signals."

St. Paul's face reddened:

"These are divine mysteries which we cannot understand, but must accept on faith. You will find that mere intellectual cleverness will not take you far up here."

After a pause he continued:

"Thirdly, you will find that there are Sessions of Praise every morning and evening. You may be surprised to hear of day and night here, now that you are no longer on a rotating earth. But we have found that sleep remains a psychological need. Humanly-formed minds still find uninterrupted consciousness too much to bear, and we have had to make a concession to that weakness. So our spiritual programme fits in with this daily rhythm: a bell will awaken you for Morning Praise, and another will summon you to Evening Praise just before darkness falls."

"Is the Praise compulsory?" asked a voice from the back row.

St. Paul's face turned a deeper shade of red. "I never thought to hear such a question from this audience", he thundered. "I would have thought that you will all *want* to praise without ceasing. But if any of you should evince the slightest reluctance, I think you will find that your guardian angel will have something to say. An internal voice will ensure that you do not want to miss a note of it."

"And since this particular intake has been so full of questions, I will mention another matter, though I would have thought it should go without saying. There will be no smoking, no alcohol, no drugs, and no sexual behavior. It is not so much that these things are not *permitted*, it is rather that they are not *possible* here." He paused.

"Now, before I open the door to heaven itself, any further questions?"

A grey arm went up in the third row.

"May I ask, sir, what we are supposed to *do* all day, apart from the Praise Sessions?" This came in a soft voice from a face hidden by waves of auburn hair.

"Do you not understand?" thundered St. Paul, "You are now in the realm of freedom. There is nothing you are *supposed* to do, except for the Praise itself. On earth you were subject to the natural laws of biologically embodied existence. You were born, you reproduced, and you died. Women had to undergo the labours of childbirth and childcare; men had to work for the bread of life; and you all had to die. Those were the terms and conditions of expulsion from the Garden of Eden - you'll find them in the small print at *Genesis* 3:16-24. But here you are free from all that."

That delightful feminine voice replied:

"I think I understand, sir. But it does not answer the question what we are to do with our time, if we are freed from those human necessities."

"As I have already said, you are *free*. You can do whatever is worth doing for its own sake. Most importantly, you can *love*."

"But what sort of love can that be?" continued that soft voice, which so held my attention. "I take it that our desire for our spouses is now ruled out. And presumably women are freed from the *rule* of their husbands, which was also mentioned in Genesis?"

St. Paul drew himself up to this full height, gathered his black gown around himself, and said in a tone that brooked no further reply:

"I suggest, miss, that you have much to learn about divine love. *That* will give you plenty to do."

I could just catch him adding in an undertone: "I never did approve of women speaking in church." Then he announced to the whole room: "That is all you need to know. If you fly out by the door opposite to that by which you entered, you will find yourselves in heaven itself."

When I got through, I emerged into a space crowded with spiritual bodies in every direction, like the stars of the sky. We were immediately dive-bombed by a swarm of tiny baby-faced fliers who buzzed round our heads with a high-pitched collective whine.

"What are these?" I asked Kevin, who had loyally stayed at my side.

"These must be the cherubim", he said. "I didn't realize they'd be so numerous, or so thin - artists made them much more cherubic. But if you think about it, there must be millions who died in childhood, especially before the industrial revolution."

"Don't they get to grow up?"

"I hope so. Wait and see."

We waved our hands at the swarm, and the cherubim flitted away. Kevin and I flew onwards, and stopped at the first ambrosia-dispenser, more from curiosity than need. And there, sipping at the golden fountain, was that wavy auburn hair I'd noticed in the lecture.

"How's the ambrosia?" I asked.

"It's very sweet. I suspect it will soon cloy," she said, with a shy smile. Her face was beautifully sad: still young, but affected by suffering.

"I'd prefer a pint of bitter", I said.

"That sounds great - but if St. Paul is to be believed, it's not available here."

"Ah yes: 'it is not that it is not permitted, it is simply not possible'."

"His very words. I have a sinking feeling we'll be hearing them again."

"Well, I suppose we must make the best of it. May we introduce ourselves? - my name's Lionel, and this is my friend Kevin."

"I'm Julia."

And we shook our grey plastic hands in a rather formal way.

Kevin said: "Let's give the ambrosia a miss. I don't feel any need for it yet, and your mention of a pint of beer has rather put me off."

"Is that to be only a nostalgic memory, then?" I said mournfully.

Julia's presence brightened the prospect, however, so I turned to her and said:

"Well, Julia, how would you like to join us on an unguided tour through heaven?"

"Goodness, I've never had such an offer before. That sounds ... well ... just heavenly", she said with a giggle.

"Come fly with us, then – though I've no idea where to."

As we buzzed around aimlessly, Kevin asked Julia: "What brings you up here so early?"

"Oh, it's a sad story. I died of kidney failure before I reached thirty. There were no transplants available, and I went out like a light. I had to leave Dave in sole charge of our two little boys, and I'm desperate to know how they're getting on."

"Of course", said Kevin, "I'm curious to know how my wife is doing, too. Perhaps she's enjoying a well-earned rest from me. ... But so far as I know, there's no communication with those we've left behind, despite the claims of the mediums. Yet I suppose news must come up from earth when new people arrive here."

"But that would be a chancy business, wouldn't it? We'd have to wait for people to die - and then how could we find them, in this crowd? I hope Dave marries again, for his own sake and for the boys. And it had better be someone who is loving *and* practical, he wasn't much good at cooking."

I said to Julia: "I thought you asked the most penetrating question at Paul's induction talk."

"Thank you, Lionel. Actually, I studied Philosophy and Theology at Edinburgh, but then Dave and I got married, and we started a family rather more quickly than we intended. And what did *you* do?"

"I was a musician."

"What instrument did you play?"

"Double bass. The lowest form of orchestral life."

"In which orchestra?"

"The Halle."

"Don't undersell yourself, then. You must have played with some great conductors."

"Yes, I've had some good experiences - and some not so good ones."

"Join the club. What more do you expect of life?"

As the three of us flew onwards, we encountered more spiritualized bodies of many shapes and sizes, colors and ages. There weren't so many older-looking ones, and Kevin came up with the explanation:

"It's only in the last century or so that average life-span has increased. For eons before that most humans were dead by forty."

Then Julia pointed out some who looked distinctly subhuman. They had huge jaws, hairy eyebrows on big eye-ridges, and receding foreheads.

"What on earth (in heaven, I mean) are those?" Julia asked nervously."

"They look like Neanderthals", I said.

"They do indeed. How very enlightened of Heaven to admit them!" said Kevin.

"But if *they* are let in, where draw the line?" I asked. "Why not our remoter cousins like the chimpanzees? And why not my cat? - I'm missing her already."

"I really don't know", said Kevin - unusually for him.

"Why don't we ask those guardian angels?" said Julia brightly.

So we located a heavenly phone box in its spherical transparent plastic, and the three of us squeezed inside. Julia sat on my lap, which was nice, but her wings tickled my nose, and I sneezed so explosively that I blew a hole in her right-hand wing.

"I'm terribly sorry, I seem to have winged you", I said.

"That's all right, I didn't feel a thing".

"But there's a hole in your wing. I'm afraid I've committed my first sin in heaven."

Kevin intervened: "I'm sure that omnipotence will have provided for such little accidents. We can ask the angel about that too."

"Your angel or mine?" said Julia.

"Oh, it doesn't matter. I expect they all give the same answer. "I said. "You try, Kevin. You were always a dab hand at new technology."

He presented his bar code to the machine, and we all listened in.

> **Welcome to Heavenly Services:**
> **please press 1 for confession,**
> **2 for spiritual direction,**
> **3 for theological questions**

Julia pressed 3.

> **For questions about earth, press 1**
> **For questions about Heaven, press 2**
> **For questions about the Trinity, press 3**
> **For all other questions, press 4**

Kevin pressed 2, and an angelic voice answered.

"Hi, Kevin, I was wondering when you'd get in touch. Welcome to Heavenly Services. My name is Gabrielle, and I am your guardian angel. How can I help you?"

"Well, Gabrielle, I'm delighted to be in contact with you at last. You must have been watching over me for some time - and may I say you've done a pretty good job."

"Thank you, Kevin, but beware of complacency."

"Yes indeed, point taken. Well, we were wondering about the Neanderthals - if that is what they are? If they are admitted, why not go further back and admit our remoter ancestors, and other animals?"

"Do I detect a whiff of species prejudice behind the question?" replied Gabrielle. "Just because people look different, you shouldn't assume they have different spiritual capacities from yourself. You can rest assured that Heavenly Management have their admissions policy under continual review."

At this point, I intervened: "With all due respect, that does not answer our question."

"Ah, someone else is listening in to this conversation? You should have informed me, Kevin. It's permitted for theological questions, although not for confessions and spiritual direction, so I'll continue ... Firstly, I should point out that it's not my function to justify all the ways of God to man. But I can tell you this much: we have a well-organized Managerial Structure here - an Assembly of Saints, a hierarchy of angels and archangels, and above all The Committee of Three. After a recent restructuring of our Management (in which, you will be reassured to know, the Top Three remain unchanged), it was decided to admit Neanderthals."

"I suppose that's the only answer we can expect", said Kevin.

Then Gabrielle added: "Before I close this conversation, I must issue a spiritual health warning: although interest in theological questions is permitted, it must never be at the cost of your own spiritual progress."

We squeezed out of the plastic sphere, and flew onwards. Julia kept veering to the right, and I realized that her damaged wing was affecting her flight-path. I offered to hold her hand to keep her on course, and she gratefully accepted. A sharp little voice inside my head said: "No sexual behavior", but then another said: "This isn't sexual, it's *friendly* behavior". A third voice said: "Can you tell the difference?" then a fourth said: "Shut up and get on with it". So we flew on, in tight formation.

Suddenly a bell-like sound arose all around us in three-dimensional space. Everyone stopped flying, and assumed an attitude of reverence. A creature with gorgeous robes and wings appeared out of nowhere.

"Ooh", whispered Kevin, "that must be an archangel. I've never seen one of them before".

We fell silent, as the archangel's glowing eyes swivelled in our direction. It raised its enormous hands, and an organ-like sound throbbed through us. The music that followed was unlike any I had heard before. There was a peculiarly breathless kind of chanting, accompanied by harp-like pluckings. Some of our fellow-fliers joined in, with their squeaky voices.

As this din went on, I scanned the congregation, and suddenly noticed a face that looked remarkably like my Dad. Could it really be him? - but why not? He should be as good a candidate for heaven as most humankind. I felt a burst of excitement, then a lump in my throat. I tried to wave to him, but those archangelic eyes turned towards me again. Then there came, familiar from school, the hymn 'Praise Him from whom all blessings flow'. Rather to my own surprise I found myself joining in. Kevin was well practiced of course, and Julia revealed a very pleasant singing voice. When the Praise ended, darkness fell rapidly, and the archangel flapped majestically away. We began to feel sleepy. As if by magic, hundreds of perching-places appeared. As we settled down and folded our wings, I said to Julia:

"Do you know, I think I saw my Dad at the Praise. He died ten years ago."

"Are you sure? How wonderful, let's try and find him tomorrow".

The whine of wings stopped, our whole flock roosted, and we fell asleep.

***

I dreamt of my pussycat - she was lying on my chest with her arms around my neck purring loudly, and I was tickling her furry cheeks. When I woke, light was dawning and our fellow-roosters were already queuing at the ambrosia-dispenser. A bell rang, and everyone assembled for Morning Praise, which made an effort to be multicultural – there was some chanting that might have been Sufi or Buddhist or Zoroastrian for all I know. Suddenly there was that familiar face again, on the other side of the central space. This time I was certain it was Dad. I waved to him, and caught his attention. He broke into a broad smile, and moved towards me, but an archangelic wing came down and blocked his path. As the chants went on, we kept sneaking looks at each other. His face was as I remembered him in his hospital bed - tired, but with considerable animation left. As soon as the Praise ended, we flew towards each other and embraced awkwardly, trying to avoid the wings on each other's backs.

"Dad", I said, through tears of joy, "I thought I'd never see you again."

For a while he couldn't speak at all. Eventually, he coughed out: "I kept hoping you'd join me up here. But I wasn't sure you'd get in."

"Well, I surprised myself on that point."

"How's Mum?"

"Oh, pretty good for her age, though she gets a bit anxious about small things. I suppose she'll soon be joining us, but you'll find her a bit failed."

"She'll remember me, surely?"

"Oh yes, she keeps talking about you."

Kevin and Julia waited politely until our first flush of emotion subsided, then came up.

"Dad, this is Kevin, my friend from Oxford. Remember, I brought him home once?"

"It rings a faint bell."

"And this is Julia, a friend we've met up here."

"Pleased to meet you, Julia. This fellow's incorrigible - still picking up new girls, even in heaven!"

Julia giggled.

"Oh Dad!" I said, "It's not like that here - haven't you noticed?"

"Isn't it? I did worry whether you'd get in here, considering the rate at which you got through your dubious women."

Julia spluttered, and Kevin grinned. I felt a sudden flash of the old irritation.

"Dad, *you're* the one who's incorrigible - still moralizing."

Kevin intervened: "Family reunions are a great blessing. I expect we can look forward to many more."

"Yes, I've already found two of my grandparents", said Dad.

"Then there'll be the great-grandparents, and great-great-grandparents, and so on," said Julia.

"Wouldn't it be fascinating to meet one's thousand-fold grandparents?" ventured Kevin.

"But if you think about it", replied Julia, "there'd be far too many of them. You couldn't remember them all."

"And there wouldn't be a language in common", I added.

"Indeed - our mother-tongue and our culture are part of our identity", said Julia, "and I was given to suppose that heaven preserves our individual identities."

Dad interrupted us: "I always felt left out of your intellectual arguments. You'll have plenty of time for them up here; but first, how about me showing you round the bits of heaven I've found so far?"

"That sounds good", said Julia, "But what shall I call you? - I can hardly call you 'Dad', can I?"

"Well, it would be nice if you did. None of Lionel's previous girls got that far."

My anger rose again: "Dad, Julia is not 'one of my girls'. You're embarrassing me - and her."

"Oh, you don't have to worry about embarrassment up here, it's all different."

"Some of it doesn't seem so different", I said, darkly.

"What about that tour of heaven, then?" said Julia, sweetly.

Dad flitted ahead and took us first to an area of white decking where there were a variety of insipid games and entertainments on offer, as on a cruise liner. There was a cinema, with a constant round of showings, "but no violence, and certainly no porn", said Dad.

"What does that leave?" I asked.

"Oh, some art films, musicals, and children's stuff. I've seen most of them already."

There was a games room, but with no gambling and no monetary rewards.

"There's no need for money in heaven. In that respect, we're all equal here", said Dad. He then fled the way to an enormous oval structure in which 3-D football was played. There was no aggression, no foul play, and no over-the-top glorying in goals. Players just complimented each other: "Oh, good shot, sir!" or "Well buzzed, there!" There was a match going on between The Angelicals and The Saints, which The Saints won, though only by a miracle. But it was a rather tame affair, and we soon took our leave. We wondered what to do next. Dad said he'd heard there was a University of the Ageless, where people could attend lectures and seminars and do research in the libraries and laboratories. Julia expressed interest, and I offered to accompany her. Kevin had seen a lot of universities already, and decided to explore other aspects of heaven with Dad. We agreed to meet at the next Evening Praise.

As Julia and I flitted hand in hand again, her damaged wing still dragging her sideways, she asked, with a smile:

"So what's all this about your dubious women?"

"Oh, Dad is impossible. He still can't let the subject rest. I could never work out how much of his attitude was disapproval, and how much was envy."

"So you *have* had quite a history."

"Well, I had a few girl-friends. They were all musicians. The back desk of basses was a good place for surveying the talent."

"In both senses of the word."

"Haha, yes. But somehow none of my relationships lasted very long. We would begin with an *allegro appassianato*, followed by a lugubrious slow movement, and a *furioso* finale."

"So you never lived with any of them?"

"Oh yes, I spent six months with Tessie in her grotty flat in Salford, until she threw me out, and last year Gretchen moved in to my place, until she got tired of me."

"No children, obviously."

"Of course. We made very sure of that."

"So you're alone now? - I mean, before you got posted up here", she added.

"I had my beloved cat. She outlasted all my girl-friends."

"What's her name?"

"Debussy."

"I should have guessed!'

A silence ensued, while we flew on in dual formation. Then Julia said:

"Lionel, may I ask how old you are? I mean, when you died?"

"Thirty-three."

"I was only twenty-five. We're both a bit premature here. And I don't know about you, but I really don't want to *be* here, I should be down *there,* bringing up my boys."

"What age are they?"

"Jason was four, and Jamie was only two."

"Very young. So they need you."

"Of course they do. They need me desperately. And I need to be with them." Tears were rolling down her cheeks. "I think Dave needs me, too. And I want to be with him, bringing up our family."

I had what seemed like a bright idea:

"Why not ring your guardian angel, and ask for a demotion?"

"I doubt whether that is possible."

"You never know. Maybe they can perform a miracle for you? They're supposed be to omnipotent, aren't they? There's no harm in asking."

So we got into the next phone-sphere, Julia dialled Heavenly Services, and the options came up as before.

"Does this count as confession, spiritual direction, or theological speculation?" she asked.

"I'm not sure. I suppose it's direction of some sort."

So she pressed 2.

"Hi, Julia, my name is Michaelis, and I am your guardian angel. I was wondering when you'd call. How can I help you today?"

"Well, Michaelis, this may be an unusual request, but you probably know that I am the mother of a young family. They badly need me, and I feel very strongly that my place is with them. So I was wondering if there is any chance of a demotion back to earth. *Please*."

There was a silence for a few moments, then the answer came:

"Julia, I sympathize with your predicament, and I'd love to be able to help, but I can't. It's not that ... '

"Oh, I know the line - 'it's not that it's not permitted, it is simply that it is not possible'."

"You have learnt one of the lessons of heaven, Julia. But you have not learnt another - that it is not done to interrupt an angel."

"Whoops! Sorry."

Then I decided to intervene: "But surely Jesus himself brought people back to life. What about Lazarus, and the centurion's daughter?

"Nobody else is supposed to listen in to spiritual direction. If this is to be a three-way conversation, I will have to switch it to category 3: Theological Questions".

"Please do", I said.

"And remember that it may be recorded for a check on orthodoxy."

"I guess we'll have to live with that. So why can't you arrange a miracle for Julia?"

"The answer lies in the distinction between resuscitation and resurrection. Lazarus and the others brought back to life by Jesus were cases of *resuscitation*. After dying, they were restored to a further period of life on earth, and later they died in one of the normal ways. But what you are now enjoying is *resurrection*, with a spiritualized body, in a new kind of space and time. And from that there can be no return."

"I'm not sure how much I'm *enjoying* it", I replied. "But if a miracle is possible in one case, why not in the other?"

"You are questioning the edicts of Heavenly Management. I therefore have to inform you that no further dialogue will be entered into on this matter."

"I knew it would be no use", said Julia disconsolately, "but it was a nice try, Lionel."

We had forgotten that the angel was still on the line: "May I point out that your wing can be repaired, Julia. That will straighten your path through heaven, and relieve you of any need for that unseemly handholding".

Michaelis directed us to a heavenly pit-stop, with a sign:

Wings repaired
seamlessly and organically

"I don't care whether my wing is repaired, I just don't want to be here, " said Julia.

"I know. But since you *are* here, and there seems to be no way back, you may as well make the best of it."

"I suppose so", she said, without enthusiasm.

So Julia was shown into a tunnel, while I waited. After a minute or so, I heard a high-pitched scream, and I rushed in. She was being lifted towards the underside of a spider about twice the size of herself. The attendants were saying:

"We pride ourselves on our organic sourcing, and arachnid silk is by far the best material for wing repair. And Nellie here has the most heavenly disposition - she wouldn't hurt a fly."

"But I can't stand the sight of spiders!" squealed Julia.

The Wing Consultant intervened: "Now, now, we know that some people find this procedure a little unpleasant, but we can't have you flying round heaven in circles, can we? I'll give you this mental anaesthetic."

But Julia shouted: "Don't I have the right to refuse treatment?"

I stepped forward, but stronger wings than mine barred the way. There were no more screams, just a sound of stitching. Then Julia came flying down the tunnel - in a perfect straight line - with a dreamy expression on her face.

"There - that wasn't so bad after all, was it?" I said. She nodded vacantly.

"We were going to look for that heavenly University, weren't we?" I said gently.

So we flitted onwards, but to my intense delight, Julia still wanted to hold my hand, despite there being no longer any aerodynamic need for it. Her hand warmed in mine, but then I felt it tremble, and soon her whole body was shaking.

"What's the matter?" I asked.

"The memory is coming back - those gleaming eyes, eight hairy legs, and that spidery silk hissing out of her belly."

"Don't worry, it's all over. And your wing is back to normal."

"My mind isn't."

"That will surely pass."

"They had no right to inflict that on me."

"I quite agree."

She was still shaking all over, so I put my arms tight around her and gave her a long hug. Suddenly a swarm of cherubim buzzed round our heads, and the Neanderthals started grunted rhythmically in the background. If the Heavenly Management's intention was to eliminate all unseemly behaviour, it seemed to be backfiring. After a while, Julia's trembling subsided, and I suggested a shot of ambrosia to restore our energies. We perched at the nearest dispenser, with my arm remaining around her back, which still registered occasional convulsions. Suddenly Kevin and Dad flew in from behind.

"Oho, you just can't leave the girls alone, even in heaven", chortled Dad.

"Dad, you misunderstand - as always. Julia's had an alarming experience."

"Haven't I heard that excuse before?"

"Dad, you're incorrigible, as *I've* said before!"

Kevin said: "Julia, you do look shaken. Surely there can't be traumatic experiences in heaven?"

"She was sectioned to undergo wing repair with silk from a live spider", I said.

"Heavenly spiders should be harmless", said Keith, "Remember Isaiah's vision of the holy mountain, where the lion will lie down with the lamb, and the child will play over the den of the asp?"

"Biologically implausible", I said.

"I can't stand spiders, heavenly or not", moaned Julia, "I think I've got post-traumatic stress."

"Well, it looks like Lionel is helping you overcome it," observed Kevin, "maybe Heaven has a hand in that too?

"What about that heavenly University? Did you come across it?" asked Dad.

"No", I said, "we got delayed by arachnophobia".

"Shall we have a look for it now?

"OK, let's flit", announced Julia, flexing her newly-repaired wing, and still holding my hand.

After a zigzag flight through heavenly space, we eventually came upon the sign:

UNIVERSITY
OF THE HEAVENLY AGE
no tuition fees
no exams
no research assessment

The four of us flew in, and made a graceful landing on a large oval lawn of perfectly-manicured grass. Some beautiful young things and well-dressed older things (all equipped with wings, of course) were lounging around, quaffing what looked like champagne. A string quartet was playing Schubert.

"I always said universities don't do any real work", pronounced Dad.

"Can that be champagne?" I said, "I thought alcohol didn't exist up here."

"Let's try it", said Keith, who felt sufficiently at home to help himself from the table.

"Ugh, it's sickly sweet, not like champagne should be", said Julia.

"I think it must be ambrosia diluted with carbonated water", said Dad. "I'd give a lot for a pint of mild."

"Now *there*, Dad, you and I agree completely". I smiled and put my arm round him. Despite the insipid nature of the drink, we enjoyed the moment. But suddenly the shadows lengthened across the lawn, an archangel flapped in over the towers, and we all had to perch to attention for Evening Praise. Then we roosted on the grass.

I dreamt of Julia. Her hair swept over me in auburn waves. Her eyes danced, and her fingers played music over my skin. Her voice modulated from sharp intelligence to playful wit and soft affection. She seemed to return several times, with increasing passion. I woke up with what felt like an eager erection - but no, it couldn't be, for I no longer had the equipment. Yet the yearning was just as strong, and in my frustration I couldn't get back to sleep.

Eventually the others woke up. The shadows retreated in that stately college garden, and my pseudo-erection faded with them. I smiled at Julia, and she smiled back in a knowing way, though how much she guessed about my state, I did not know. The Morning Praise included a chorus from Handel's *Messiah*.

"Well, the musical standard's going up" I said. "Do you think we'll get excerpts from Bach's *B Minor Mass*, Mozart's *Requiem*, Elgar's *Dream of Gerontius*, Mahler's *Resurrection Symphony*, or Britten's *War Requiem*?

"What a name-dropper you are", said Dad.

"Some of those works are more musical than spiritual", observed Kevin.

"How can such great music not be spiritual?" I asked.

"I suspect Heavenly Management may find your taste a bit too elitist", said Julia.

"Wouldn't you like a change from those blessed harps?"

She giggled, but I suspected she might be right about the Management's attitude.

After a light breakfast (of ambrosia, of course) we began to explore the heavenly university and discovered the lecture list, which read:

> **Noah: How to survive environmental catastrophe
> (a message for our times)
> Joshua: The military conquest of Canaan
> (another message for our time)s
> Ruth: How to find a good husband
> Job: When times get hard, don't try theology
> Isaiah: Prophecy for beginners
> Jeremiah: Prophecy for depressives
> Professor Paul: Why my theology is justified by faith
> Professor James: The need for hard work
> Professor Augustine: Confessions of a North African Bishop
> Professor Thomas Aquinas: The Summa Theologica revisited
> (576 lectures, followed by a beatific vision)
> Ayatollah Al-Ghazali: Why the philosophers are still incoherent
> Rabbi Maimonides: Guidance for those who are still perplexed
> Professor C.S.Lewis: The four loves**

"Fascinating", exclaimed Kevin, "I'd like to hear all of them."

"Even the 576 by St.Thomas? I hope there's a shorter path to the beatific vision", said Julia.

"I see they've gone for political correctness: there's a token woman, a token Jew, and a token Muslim", I remarked.

"Technically, Joshua, Isaiah and Jeremiah were all Jews", commented Keith.

"Well, you know what I mean", I said. "Which lecture shall we go to today?"

Dad said, "I don't care, as long as it's not the 576."

Keith remarked: "We have all eternity before us, so we can hear them all in due course."

"Oh God, please no!" said Dad.

"You have freewill. You can go back to the games whenever you want", said Kevin.

"You choose for us today", I suggested to Julia.

"What about C.S.Lewis, then? I once read some of his stuff, and he had a delightful style, even if I didn't buy his metaphysics. I was going to read his Narnia stories to my boys when they were older. I'd love to see him in the flesh - if this grey stuff counts as flesh."

So we found the right lecture-theatre, and perched on the benches. Being a bit early, we waited in profound silence while others flitted in with solemn expressions on their faces. An ancient-looking clock ticked, until the theatre was about half-full. At 10.05 precisely a hatch opened high up in the wall, and a figure in black appeared. He flew down slowly, encased in a long black gown. There were holes for his wings, but the gown trailed below and behind him, and must have caused some wind resistance. He flapped to the lectern, where he gathered his folds around him.

"I see I am due to speak on the four loves", he said, in a formal but pleasant voice. "I did commit a book on this subject in my earthly life. And I am honoured to say that it is one of those that have been given the *imprimatur* up here. This is a great privilege, for the Heavenly Librarians are very careful about what they admit. Much literature - and not a little theology - is deemed unsuitable. But my little effort, I am pleased to say, is eternally there for your perusal. Therefore, if you will permit me, I will just give you a brief outline of the main ideas this morning."

"What if we don't permit you?" asked some wag in the back row.

"My phrase was rhetorical, sir", answered Professor Lewis, "and in this Place, above all, you should learn some rhetoric - and some manners."

"Now, my basic theme is that there are three main kinds of human love, and on a different level there is a fourth love which is divine. You all know about erotic attraction (*eros* in the Greek). Indeed, for some of you that may be practically the only kind of love you ever think about."

A snigger somewhere in the audience.

"But by *eros* I do not mean mere lust - raw sexual desire. Even the animals have that, but we are capable of something more, which is manifested in a desire to spend one's time - perhaps all one's life - with someone. It is the sort of love we mean when we talk of 'falling in love'. Obviously, there can be lust without love. And though falling in love typically involves sexual desire (call it lust if you must), the latter is only one component in the mix. The middle-aged like myself, are still capable of falling in love, perhaps even when they are getting a bit beyond lust."

Julia whispered to me: "He fell in love with an American lady and married her, and then she died of cancer. I do hope they've found each other again here".

Meanwhile our Professor was saying: "Plato and Dante held that *eros* can be spiritualized into something divine - and I am inclined to think they are right. The second kind of human love", he continued, "is perhaps best called affection (the Greek word for it is *sorge*). Think of the love of parents for their children, and vice versa, and of the love of siblings for each other. But it is not confined to families - you might feel affection for some of your teachers, and for old acquaintances. Nor is it confined to people: we can feel affection for our pets, for places, for our houses, perhaps even for a car. Of these, of course, only the animals (dogs more than cats, I think) feel anything like affection in return."

"He doesn't know Debussy", I whispered.

"The third kind of human love", Professor Lewis continued, raising his voice a notch, "is friendship (*philia*). Aristotle famously wrote about it. Unlike affection, this can only be between persons who treat each other as equals. It may be possible for people of different social status to be friends - a landowner and his gamekeeper, for example - but if so, they must treat each other as equals within that relationship. Friendship is not biologically based, like eros and affection. In this sort of love, humans begin to transcend their biology.

"Finally, we come to divine love (*agape* in the Greek). In the King James Bible this was translated as 'charity' - some of you may remember hearing of the three theological virtues, faith, hope and charity - but that traditional usage has become obsolete and misleading. *Agape* is the love of God for Man, and of Man for God."

Julia put her hand up: "What about women?"

"Yes, the young ladies always ask that these days. I am using the term 'Man' in the generic sense. I should have thought that was obvious."

"But why not use one of the alternatives, such as 'persons', 'people', 'humans', 'humankind'? replied Julia.

Clives Staples Lewis looked her in the eye, and said, not unkindly: "Charity might suggest that you might allow me to be a man of my time. Now, where were we? Oh yes, *agape*. It is not confined to God. We can also show to it each other. When Jesus commanded us to love our neighbours as ourselves, he obviously did not mean erotic love (that would be inconvenient - or worse) nor did he merely mean affection or friendship. We cannot feel these for everyone, nor do we feel them for ourselves. *Agape* is more like wanting the very best for someone. That, of course, raises the huge question what really *is* best - but that deserves a course of lectures to itself. You may find the topic on the list in future, and I would commend it to you. Today I will leave you with the thought that our human loves, though good in themselves, are liable to corruption. They need to be kept sweet by an admixture of *agape*, which is transcendent and divine. Hence our need for regular spiritual practice."

He paused, and looked at us quizzically. "I see there is time for a question or two", he said. "Are there any enquiring minds out there?"

I put up a hand: "Can more than one of these loves be present in the same relationship?"

"Oh yes, certainly - and quite often. That was implicit in what I said. Admittedly, affection for a cat or a car can hardly be conceived of as involving *friendship*, but even there, something may sometimes be needed to stop such affections becoming unbalanced or obsessive."

"Can't marriage involve all four loves?" put in Julia.

"Of course. And that is just as it should be."

That hit me like a revelation - of the blindingly obvious, like all the best revelations. With Tessie and Gretchen and the others, there was *eros* and lust, and not only on my side, unless I was much deceived. I wouldn't say there was *no* element of friendship or affection, or even of wishing the best for each other (though I could hardly say that anything divine came into it), but clearly there was not enough. My relationships had been unbalanced: when *eros* cooled, there wasn't much else to keep them going. But for Julia, now, I realized that I felt all four loves at once.

We left the lecture-theatre thoughtfully. Dad remarked: "I actually understood most of that. It sounded like common sense."

"So maybe there is point in universities, after all?" said Kevin.

"It might be dangerous to generalize from one example", said Julia.

For the moment, reeling from my revelation, I was lost for words. Then Julia pointed to the black-gowned Professor Lewis flapping over the roof-tops, arm-in-arm with a smartly-dressed lady.

"Look!" she exclaimed delightedly, he's found his dead wife! Perhaps they can now enjoy all the four loves together."

"I thought *eros* was not permitted up here", I said.

"I know they said that", said Kevin, "but this makes me wish they didn't mean it."

"What - you of all people, doubting the Word of Heaven?"

"We can always discuss its correct interpretation."

Dad then announced: "Well, that's enough intellectual discussion for one day. I feel like some games - or maybe hunting down some more ancestors. See you at the Praise." And off he winged.

Kevin said: "I rather fancy taking in some more of those lectures. There are so many famous speakers I never got the chance to hear on earth."

"See you in 576 days' time, then", said Julia, "and better allow one more for the beatific vision".

Julia and I were left alone together, and I suggested a flit round the college garden. There was a pregnant silence between us as we circled exotic shrubs and trees. We perched on a branch resplendent in fragrant pink blossom.

"That's the first smell I've noticed in heaven", said Julia.

"Yes, there isn't very much for the senses to enjoy here, is there?"

Another silence followed. Then I suddenly found myself saying: "Julia, there's something I have to tell you."

"Yes?" she said, playfully.

"I love you."

"I thought that was not permitted here!"

"They say it is not even *possible*, but it seems to me it is."

She broke into the most beautiful smile I had ever seen.

"Whatever they say ... Lionel, I think I feel something of the impossible too."

We kissed. We still had lips and tongues, even if other equipment was missing. That someone like her should love someone like me seemed the greatest miracle of all. But it wasn't long before our ecstasy was interrupted by a tremendous whirr as a swarm of buzzing cherubim surrounded our tree. They came in through the branches and perched around us, pointing and giggling. We were so infuriated that I decided to phone Heavenly Services and register a complaitn. My guardian angel replied quickly:

"Hi, Lionel, my name is Chrisalis. I was thinking it is high time you got in touch, for it is already your third day in heaven. How can I help you?"

"Well, Chrisalis, I've been quite busy - as you probably know. But I want to register a complaint. Why can't we enjoy a private kiss without being disturbed by these sex-crazed babes?"

"It is my duty to tell you, Lionel, there are several points to make about that. Firstly, your complaint suggests some degree of prejudice, which is not supposed to exist in heaven. Secondly, no kiss is of purely private significance: for every relationship affects other people too. 'No man is an island', as one of your poets wrote. Thirdly, there are kisses of blessing, of greeting, and of friendly affection, but erotic kisses are not expected here."

Then Julia broke in with what seemed to me a very pertinent theological question:

"Why can't these cherubim move on from where they've got stuck? I thought the point of heaven was to enable *everyone* to make spiritual progress."

"Your question, Julia, is a deep one. There is no completely satisfactory solution, and Heavenly Management keeps the matter under constant review. The problem is that spiritual progress cannot be guaranteed. There needs to be some movement on the part of the creature, before grace can be added. Therein lies the mystery of freewill. It may seem that some minds are so unformed that they cannot make even the minimum effort that is necessary. But in this matter not even the Committee of Three can tell what is possible. It depends on human relationships: for example, children need parents who love them as individuals, if they are to grow in grace. But love is not something we can enforce."

"So there is a problem of evil even in heaven", said Julia.

"Given freedom, that is a logical corollary", said the angel.

It was time for me to put in *my* pennyworth: "I want you to know, Chrisalis, that I have had a sort of revelation - you can call it spiritual progress if you like. I have realized how the different kinds of love can be united in marriage. So why can't we be allowed to act on that here?"

Chrisalis said: "The answer lies with Heavenly Decree. In heaven there is no marriage and no giving in marriage. And certainly no *eros* outside marriage."

"What a depressing conclusion", I said, and rang off.

Julia and I flew disconsolately round the garden again. The blessed cherubim had disappeared, but we knew that as soon as we embraced or kissed they would buzz us again.

"What about Dave?" it occurred to me to say.

"Oh, I still love him. But my intuition tells me he'll be looking for a replacement."

"But what about your marriage vows?"

"As I remember, the wording was 'until death do us part'. And we've already established that there is no going back."

"Well, Julia, if I ever have children, I would like you to be their mother."

"That is probably the nicest compliment I've ever had, Lionel. But as the angel said, it's not possible here."

We kissed again, passionately. Immediately there was a buzz from over the trees. I broke off and said: "This is just too frustrating. There's enough of us left to arouse *eros*, but not enough to consummate it."

"Yes", said Julia, "we can't go on meeting like this."

"But how can we stop?" I replied.

Suddenly I had an idea. On the impulse, I phoned up Chrisalis again, and said:

"We'd like to commit *Liebestod*, please."

"What was that word? - I may have to consult a German-speaking angel. I'm sure we have one somewhere."

"You needn't bother. It means *love-death* - the kind of love that can only be fulfilled in death, as in Wagner's *Tristan and Isolde*."

"Wagner? You can be pretty sure *he's* not up here - though some of his music is. But you must surely realize that there's no death here. It's not that it's not permitted, it is just that it is impossible."

Julia sighed: "That line all over again."

"I'm afraid the impossible is just what we want", I said.

"In that case, I see nothing for it but to send you both for an interview with the Heavenly Headmaster", said Chrisalis.

We both exclaimed, simultaneously: "Oh, my God!"

"I didn't say that the Headmaster *is* God. I can neither confirm nor deny that hypothesis", replied the angel.

At that point Julia burst into spontaneous song, to a well-known hymn tune. The words started off like something from Monty Python, but then diverged:

> O Lord, please do not toast us
> Or burn us on the fire,
> You surely wouldn't do that,
> We're told how good you are.
>
> We are imperfect creatures
> Who make you feel so sore,
> But we sometimes rise above it,
> Please help us to do more.
>
> And Lord, please do not bore us
> Or keep us hanging round,
> When we've had enough existence
> Then let us go to ground.
>
> Thy kingdom come *on earth*, He said,
> Let *agape* abound;
> But if no love in fullness
> We want no second round.